Truly, Madly

Annabelle Willis

Contents

Prologue

P rologue

Four years ago

"Jade, Juliette, aren't you girls ready yet? We're hosting the party. We should go there early," said Jaden Meyers to his two sisters, Juliette Meyers who was a year older than him and Jade Meyers who was only sixteen. It was his 21st birthday and he had invited all his friends to his old classmate Dustin Moore's restaurant and bar to celebrate.

"We're ready, let's go," said Juliette and Jade, walking towards the main door.

"Dad, we're leaving," shouted Juliette from the door.

"Enjoy but not too much drinking. And you know what time to return home," said their dad. "Take care of Jade, please," said Christopher Meyers, their dad, who had retired as a lawyer, handing his law firm to his oldest son, Jayson Meyers. Jayson was away on a case and couldn't attend the birthday celebrations.

They trooped out to Jaden's RAM 2500 and climbed in. They soon were on their way to the venue.

"Just how many friends did you invite, Jady?" Asked Juliette.

"Around 25, but please don't call me that in front of everyone," he said, glaring at Juliette.

"Why am I even going?" Said Juliette, rolling her eyes.

"Please Jules, don't be a spoilsport," grumbled Jaden as he parked the truck in the parking lot of Dustin's restaurant.

It was a picture perfect little restaurant painted in white, with it's glass doors and windows. Two white lanterns hung on either side of the white panelled glass door. Jade liked the simple beauty of the place. She hated loud, harsh and extravagantly decorated bars and restaurants but this one stood out in its simplicity.

She picked a small pink buttercup from a flower pot near the door and followed the others inside. She fixed the flower to her long cascading golden locks that reached to her waist. The interiors had been tastefully decorated with white chairs and tables. Each table had a small vase of buttercups, hydrangeas and roses. There was a big birthday banner put up for Jaden. He didn't want any more birthday decorations.

She bumped into someone while staring at the decorations. "Oops sorry," she said, looking at whom she bumped into.

He stared at her without a blink and stood there just holding her waist lightly, to stop her stumble. His dark chocolate brown piercing eyes, his sharp chiseled jawline, unshaven stubble, and short chocolate brown hair made him look very gorgeous. She could feel his muscles where her hand touched his arm to arrest her fall.

"I I'm sorry, I didn't s see yyou," she stammered again but he kept on staring, as if in a trance. Her cheeks coloured and she released her hold on him.

"Oh, there you are," said Jaden. "Oh, you two have met already? Still, Jade, meet Dustin Moore, the owner of this place," he introduced. "Dustin, this is Jade, my little sister. She just turned 16."

Dustin's hand left her waist. He gave her a small nod in acknowledgement and disappeared with Jaden. Jade stood there mesmerised by him, by his touch. He was of Jaden's age, she knew as he was Jaden's classmate at school. She heard that he dropped out of school in his final year when his parents died. He had to clear all their debts as well as take care of an ailing grandmother.

He and his grandmother sold their sprawling house and bought this small property at the marketplace of their hometown, Travis Springs in Hays county, Texas. They turned it into a restaurant with a bar, naming it Jenny's Restaurant and Bar.

They cleared their dues with the rest of the money. At the backside of the restaurant they lived in two small bedrooms, with a bathroom to share. It was all they could afford.

Jenny's restaurant and bar catered to parties and get-togethers and also provided home deliveries. It provided good, wholesome meals at affordable prices, carving a name for itself over the last few years.

Jaden's friends came pouring in. They all wished Jaden, hugging him and fist bumping with him. Jade stuck with Juliette and they sat with some of the girls that Jaden had invited. They all were Jaden's school and college friends.

The cake was brought in and cut. Jade and Juliette stood next to Jaden as he cut the cake. They fed him a piece. Jade could feel Dustin's eyes on her throughout the cake cutting ceremony. Whenever she looked up at him, he looked away.

She moved away when Jaden's friends smeared the rest of the cake on his face. She went to the washroom to wash her hands. She had just reached the corridor when a husky voice arrested her.

"You have cake on your mouth too," he said and she turned around to find none other than Dustin Moore, standing in her personal space.

"Oh," she said, shyly. He was so handsome and so brave. He handled everything that came his way so well. She couldn't believe that he followed her out of the party. Was she crushing on him already? Maybe. She was just 16. She was surprised that a twenty-one year old entrepreneur would talk to her.

"Here, let me," he said, raising his hand to wipe the cake from her mouth. His thumb brushed her lower lip to wipe the cream away, causing a tingling sensation all over her. His piercing brown eyes took in her reaction to his touch.

"T T Thank you," she said, blushing furiously and lowering her eyes.

"You're very beautiful. The most beautiful girl, I've ever seen," he whispered.

"I got to go," she whispered back.

She blushed more and ran into the washroom, closing it as her heartbeat thundered in her chest. She might be falling for him. She didn't have much experience with men. She wasn't interested in her rowdy classmates. Being soft natured and gentle she stayed away from them. So when Dustin touched her, she felt strange emotions in her very soul. Emotions she never felt before.

She came out of the washroom and returned back to the party. All the time she could feel Dustin's eyes upon her, but the moment she turned to check, he looked away.

The party was a huge success. Liquor was served in moderation. Jade didn't touch it as she was just 16. Even Juliette didn't drink to give her company.

The food was very good and everyone praised Dustin for his efforts. He brought his grandma from the kitchen and introduced her to everyone. She was the one who helped cook up the dishes. All the food served were her recipes actually.

Afterwards, when the guests started leaving, Dustin led his grandma towards Jade who was busy helping the attendants clear the mess the guests had made. It wasn't her duty to do it but she was a very sweet, gentle and helpful girl. She helped anyone and everyone without asking. That was her nature.

"Granny, this is Jade, she's Jaden's sister," he said, blushing a little.

"Oh, aren't you a darling? How old are you, sweetheart?" His grandma asked.

"I'm sixteen, granny," she said, shyly, looking at granny's happy face.

Granny touched her cheek and pulled her into a hug. "God has made you with so much care. He's taken his time, I can see. You're beautiful, both inside and outside, " said granny, hugging her tightly.

"Thank you granny," she said, blushing. She felt oddly self-conscious with Dustin's eyes never leaving her face.

"Leave it, they will clean everything, " she said, leading her towards the kitchen. "Come, I have something special for you," she said.

"What granny?" Jade asked.

Granny went to a glass showcase and brought out a batch of chocolate walnut brownies, and packed them up for her.

"This is for you, sweetheart. My special batch of brownies," said grandma, handing her the pack.

Jade squealed with delight. She hugged granny and thanked her profusely. Dustin stood staring, mesmerised by her. Granny didn't miss the way her grandson stared at the young girl. She beamed with happiness at the prospect of a future grand daughter-in-law.

They came out of the kitchen and found a worried Juliette looking for her. She smiled with relief upon seeing her. They all thanked Dustin and his grandma and left.

Jade couldn't forget Dustin. She couldn't concentrate on anything. His piercing brown eyes followed her even in her dreams. She felt a weird longing to see him, to be in his arms, to talk to him, to hold his hand. She couldn't understand the feeling at all and became restless as ever.

There had to be a way to meet him again. She would die if she didn't see him again.

Chapter One

F our years ago (continued)

     Three days went by and Jade was restless as ever. So, when Jaden called her from his college dormitory in Austin to go to Dustin's restaurant and pay for the party expenses, she was ecstatic. She had to take the money from their dad and hand it over to his granny at his restaurant.

"Please don't give a cheque, Dustin's at Dallas on work and his grandma needs the money immediately, " said Jaden and Jade's face fell. So she wouldn't get to meet him? She felt like her heart would break.

"Ok," she said, quietly.

Jaden disconnected the call, relieved that the money would reach when Dustin's grandma needed it the most.

He called Dustin and informed him that Jade would go to his restaurant and hand it over to his grandma on her way back from school. Dustin thanked him and disconnected the call.

He had to go back to Travis Springs and see Jade. He would come back later for his work. He drove his old Ford F-150 as fast as possible. He had to reach his restaurant by lunchtime.

Excited beyond words at the prospect of meeting Jade, he reached his restaurant in record time, to see her car parked in front of his restaurant. Her chauffeur was sitting inside, waiting patiently for her.

The truth was ever since he saw her at Jaden's party, he was obsessed with her. He wanted to see her innocent angelic face again and again. He knew she was very young, and he shouldn't corrupt her but he was helpless. He just couldn't keep his eyes off her.

He rushed inside to see her hug his granny. Oh, what he would do to get a hug from her. He stood transfixed at the door, watching her talking to his granny. She handed his granny the envelope containing the money that her dad sent.

His granny looked at him with a surprised expression. "Weren't you in Dallas? How did you come so early?" She asked suspiciously.

"I had something important to do," he said, lowering his eyes lest his granny saw through him. She was shrewd and could read him like an open book. How? He had no idea.

His granny smiled knowingly and looked at Jade who was looking at her grandson shyly. "You must be hungry, sweetheart. Come, I have just the thing for you," she said leading her towards the back of the restaurant to Dustin's room. Dustin followed them inside too unsure what his granny was upto.

"This is Dustin's room. Sit here. I'll get you something to eat," she said leaving the room. Jade looked around the neatly arranged, clean room. It wasn't big but it was comfortable. A double bed with a dresser and a nightstand on either side of it occupied one side of the room. On the other side, there was a wardrobe and chest of drawers and a small desk.

He sat on his bed and patted the place beside him,"Sit please," he said. She sat down awkwardly, a little further away from the place where he indicated.

"Weren't you away in Dallas?" She asked him.

"Yeah, I came home to see you," he said, staring at her.

Her heart started hammering in her chest, fast. She looked up at him, stunned by his words. "Why?" She asked, hesitantly.

"Didn't you want to see me?" He asked, leaning down to her level to get a good look into her eyes.

She lowered her eyes. Oh God, what would she answer? "I I don't know," she lied, trying to avoid his questioning look.

His forefinger went under her chin and uplifted her face to his level. "Tell me that you didn't want to see me. Tell me that your heart isn't beating as fast as mine. Tell me Jade, why am I going crazy for you?" He asked, his face showing how tortured he was feeling.

"Yes, I wanted to see you," she said, searching his eyes.

Dustin simply stared at her upturned face. No, he shouldn't kiss her. She was just sixteen. She was innocent. She was untouched. She wasn't an adult yet. It would be wrong. He controlled himself as much as he could.

"Lunch is served," his granny's call aroused him from his trance.

"Come let's eat," he said, getting up and leading the way to a room where there was a modular kitchen in one corner with a four seater dining table.

There was a TV and sofas on the other side. It looked clean, cosy and very comfortable.

They sat at the table and her granny brought two plates of spaghetti with Italian Meatballs dunked in sauce. A heavenly aroma wafted into her nostrils.

They hungrily attacked the delicious food. "Mmmmm, this is heavenly," Jade said as Dustin stared at her mouth.

"Granny won't you eat with us?" She asked granny who was cleaning up.

"Not now sweetheart. I had a late breakfast," she said.

"You sit down granny. I'll clean up," said Jade.

"Oh no no. You're a real darling. Enjoy your food. It's my daily job, it's nothing I can't manage," said his granny with a chuckle.

Jade finished her plate and took it to the sink. She washed the few utensils that were there. Dustin sat watching her, mesmerised by her, laughing with his granny and doing the dishes. It seemed as if she belonged here, to his little world. Granny discreetly noticed his hypnotized state many times and chuckled inwardly. It was obvious that he was whipped with the young girl.

"I need to get going granny. I have homework to do," she said and granny hugged her.

"Ok sweetheart but do come down sometimes to see your old granny," she said kissing her cheek.

"Yes granny, I will, " Jade promised, kissing granny's cheek too.

Dustin watched them longingly and when Jade turned to leave, he jumped up and led her outside.

"When can I see you again?" He asked her and she smiled shyly.

"Will you come tomorrow again?" He asked tentatively.

"Not tomorrow, I have extra classes till 4 o'clock in the afternoon," she said.

"Oh, aren't you in Travis High?" he asked.

"Yeah. Even you and Jaden studied there," she said.

He nodded. "So when will I get to see you again?" He asked.

"I'll come down during the weekend, Saturday afternoon?" she promised.

"I'll wait for you, " he said and she nodded with a blush.

"Bye," she said.

"Bye," he sighed. She climbed into her car and left. Dustin drove to Dallas to get his work done.

Next day, Dustin fidgeted around all morning. He just couldn't get any work done. He wanted to see Jade. He wanted to talk to her, to see her face, her smile. So by 3 o'clock he drove to Travis High and waited opposite the main gate patiently.

Just one look at her wouldn't do any harm. At 4 o'clock Jade came out with a scowl. It was not in her nature to scowl. Something was wrong, he was sure.

He saw that a bunch of rowdy guys were following her passing rude remarks at her. He was furious. Getting down from his truck, he strode towards them, with his hands clenched into his fists.

"Leave Jade alone, " he growled and the boys stared at him.

Jade walked up to him and stood beside him, thankful for his intervention.

"Do you want to be suspended for bullying a girl? I could report all of you to the authorities," he said and the boys looked scared.

"Sorry sir. It won't happen again," one of them said. The others also agreed and apologised.

Dustin led Jade outside. "Do you have your car?" He asked her and she shook her head.

"No, dad's gone out in it. I'll take the bus," she said.

"Come, I'll drop you," said Dustin and Jade climbed in.

Dustin stopped in front of her house. "Thank you for saving me from those rowdy boys," she said.

Dustin grinned. "That won't do, you have to thank me nicely," he said and Jade stared at him in confusion.

"Nicely?" She asked.

"Yes, kiss me," he said, tapping on his cheek. She blushed crimson.

"That's not a good idea, " she said.

"It is a very good idea," he coaxed her.

Jade went forward and kissed his cheek. "Thank you, " she said and opening the door of his truck, jumped out and hurried home with her face burning with embarrassment.

Dustin sat as if in a daze. That innocent kiss turned him into a puppet in her hands. He knew it was wrong of him to ask for a kiss but he just lost his senses when around her.

Chapter Two

Jade couldn't sleep the next two days. Dustin's words kept ringing in her ears.

Tell me Jade, why am I going crazy for you

Kiss me

She thought them over and over and blushed everytime she remembered the kiss. She couldn't wait for tomorrow when she would go to see him in the afternoon as promised.

Unable to sleep, she took out her pocket notebook and scribbled,

I love you Dustin

I will always love you Dustin

I'm in love with you Dustin

Smiling happily at being able to express her feelings, she wrote in the next page,

To my Dustin,

I love you more than words can showI think about you more than you could ever know Until forever this will be trueBecause there is no one I could ever loveThe way I love you.

Eternally yoursJade

She smiled happily at the little poem that she wrote. Keeping the notebook away, she went into blissful sleep, dreaming about Dustin.

The next day, she was restless the whole day. After lunch she asked her dad if she could go to meet old granny Jenny.

Her dad gave her permission and she took out her bike and sped down to the marketplace. Parking her bike, she saw Dustin watching her from inside the glass windows.

She went inside and smiled at Dustin. He gestured towards the kitchen and she straight went to the kitchen without a word as there were customers in his restaurant.

Granny was busy directing the chefs, yet she smiled at her and embraced her. "Just give me five minutes, sweetheart," she said.

"May I help granny?" She asked and granny smiled appreciatively.

"You want to help me? Thank you sweetheart," granny said handing her the cake mixture. "Here, can you mix this batter to a creamy, fluffy consistency?"

"Yes granny," said Jade, doing what granny asked her to do.

Granny walked to the oven to adjust the temperature with a smug expression on her face. Jade might be young, but she was the perfect girl for her Dustin. Dustin finished at the cash counter and when granny came to take over, he came into the kitchen to see Jade.

"Wow, you can bake?" He asked as he watched her pour the cake mixture expertly into the pan and place it in the preheated oven.

"Yeah, I can cook also," she said, looking at him.

"That's wonderful. I can't wait to taste your cooking," he said, staring at her face.

"Next time I will make something and bring it for you," she said, looking up at him.

"Next time will be when?" He asked her softly.

"Let's see, " she said.

Dustin went back to the cash counter to handle billing of more customers who came in. Granny came back to the kitchen to handle their orders. Jade helped too. When all the customers left and Dustin could relax a little, he came into the kitchen.

Granny said to them,"Go home to our kitchen and eat the cake that Jade baked for us. Leave a piece for me too." Dustin nodded and led Jade to the backside of the restaurant. He opened his apartment door and they went to the kitchen with the cake.

He served themselves and brought it to the table. "This is too good," he said, helping himself to the piece.

"Thank you, but I just stirred the batter and baked it. Granny did the rest," she said, honestly.

"Still it's the best," he said, looking at her.

"Why?" She asked.

"Obviously. Because you made it," he said, still looking at her.

"Oh," she said, her cheeks turning red.

"Your girlfriend can't cook?" She asked, shyly. She wanted to know whether he had a girlfriend. He was 21 and so good looking. Surely he had a girlfriend.

Dustin chuckled at her question. Leaning closer to her, he said,"I don't have a girlfriend."

"Oh," she said, looking down to avoid his stare. She was so relieved that he didn't have a girlfriend.

He held her chin and made her look up at him. "When will I see you again?" He asked in earnest.

"Maybe next week. My dad won't give me permission so soon," she said. He nodded in understanding but how would he wait till next week?

"Can I come to see you then?" He asked her, staring at her upturned face with longing.

"Yes, please," she said and he smiled. "I've got to go home now." He nodded.

She got up and left. Dustin was about to leave and go back to his restaurant when he saw a small pocket notebook lying on the chair where she was sitting.

He wanted to rush out and give it to her, when he changed his mind. He would go to her school on Monday to return it. Grinning happily, he just flicked through the pages.

He stood frozen when he read what she had written. She loved him? He stared incredulously at the notebook. His heart sang and he did a happy dance. He just couldn't believe it that she really loved him.

"Is that a happy dance that you're doing?" Said his granny, chuckling. She grinned ear to ear at having caught her grandson do a happy dance. It sure had something to do with Jade.

"I actually, well yeah, it is. So what? Can't a guy dance in peace?" He said, blushing and going out, clutching the notebook to his chest like some treasure.

Jade came back home but couldn't find her notebook anywhere. Where did it go? It was in the pocket of her denims all the time. Where could she have dropped it? What would happen if someone found it and read it?

She had to get it. She saw that her dad was out. It was getting dark but she had to retrieve her notebook somehow. She sneaked out with her bike and rode to Dustin's restaurant again.

She saw many trucks in the restaurant's parking lot. She walked inside and saw that a fight was going on at the bar. Four drunk men were fighting amongst themselves. Dustin tried to intervene but no one listened to him. The bar became empty as the other customers left due to the gruesome fight. Suddenly one of the men took out a pistol from his waistband and pulled the trigger at one of his friends. The man fell to the ground with a thud.

Before she could scream, someone placed a hand on her mouth and pulled her away quietly towards the backside of the restaurant.

Chapter Three

Jade struggled against her abductor. Why was he taking her away? She had to go to Dustin instead she was taken to Dustin's small living area and kitchen.

"Thank you Richardson, for bringing her here safely," said granny, with a white tensed face.

"What were you doing there Jade? If you had screamed, you would have been dead by now," scolded granny. The man, Richardson, left to go back to the restaurant.

Jade came out of her shock. "I have to go granny. Dustin's there. They're going to kill him. Please granny, can't you see that I have to save him?" She yelled in panic.

"Calm down honey. The police are here. You can't go there," said granny.

"No, I have to go there. They'll hurt Dustin. Please granny, let me go. I beg of you, granny. Let me go," she pleaded with folded hands.

"Jade, come to your senses. You can't go there," said granny in a loud and firm voice.

With tears streaming down her face Jade shouted,"I love him granny. I can't live without him. I have to save him. Open the door. Oh Dustin," she said, and lost consciousness. Granny caught her and lay her down on the sofa. Her heart bled for the young girl who loved her grandson so much.

"Granny, come quickly. The police are arresting Dustin for the murder of the man he didn't commit," screamed a panicked Richardson as he came running frantically to inform granny.

Granny locked the door and went with Richardson. She was trembling after hearing the shocking news. She asked Richardson to call Jade's dad. She rushed to the police officers who were handcuffing Dustin.

"What are you doing officer? That's my grandson. He's not the murderer. We only run this restaurant and bar. Why are you arresting him?" She asked trying to free Dustin.

He was the only family she had. He was innocent, why couldn't they see it?

"We're just doing our duty, Mrs Moore. Please don't intervene. The culprit was caught red handed with the murder weapon in his hand," said the officer with a stoic face.

"If I murder someone and place the gun in your hand and escape, would that make you the culprit, officer?" She asked him. He looked confused but soon regained his composure.

"You can contend in court. But right now I'm just doing my job," the officer said.

"Is your job to arrest the innocent while the guilty flee the crime scene?" She asked, trying to stop them.

Christopher Meyers came rushing inside. "What's going on? Why are you arresting him?" He asked.

"We're arresting this man in charges of murder," said the officer.

"My grandson did not commit the murder," yelled granny.

"Leave it granny. They won't listen. The man who actually committed the murder has high political connections. He just framed me. He took advantage of my shocked state and placed the gun in my hands and fled. His accomplice shot down the CCTV camera and fled too," said Dustin, in a hoarse voice.

"I will have you bailed son, don't worry," said Jade's dad.

The officers took Dustin away and granny lost consciousness too.

When Jade woke up, she was lying in her bedroom, on her bed. Was it a bad dream or did she really witness a murder?Dustin. What happened to Dustin? She remembered that she was at the back of the restaurant in Dustin's apartment. She was pleading with granny. What happened? How did she arrive here?

She got up and ran downstairs to see her father. It was morning which could only mean one thing. She had slept through the night.

She found her dad at the table, drinking coffee and holding his head in his hands.

"Dad, dad, how did I come here?" She asked.

"I brought you home," he said, dejectedly.

"Dustin, what happened to Dustin?" She asked and her dad looked down at his coffee, silently debating whether to tell her or not.

"Dad, you've got to tell me what happened. Where's Dustin? I'm going to see him," she said, getting up.

"Sit down Jade," he said, firmly.

Jade sat down,"Then tell me dad what happened to Dustin?" She pleaded.

"The police arrested Dustin on charges of murder. Apparently the murderer has political connections and escaped, placing the gun in Dustin's hands when he was in a shocked state," said her dad.

Jade sat down on the nearest chair in shock. They arrested him?

"I've witnessed the murder dad. I was there when it happened. I know Dustin didn't do it. I saw it with my own eyes. I can recognise the man who did it. I'm going to the police to tell them," said Jade.

"No Jade, you won't go anywhere. Another witness who had come forward to give testimony has gone missing. I don't want to lose you," said her dad.

"But dad, we have to save Dustin. Is he still in police custody?" She asked.

"Yeah, I'll see if we can bail him today," said her dad.

Christopher Meyers tried his level best but could not bail Dustin. Murder was a non-bailable offence and it seemed that the real culprit hid his tracks well. Jade was heartbroken. She wanted to go and see Dustin but her dad did not let her go to the police station.

She wasn't allowed to go to the restaurant also as the police were all over the place hunting for evidence. All the evidence had disappeared overnight.

For the next two weeks, Christopher Meyers tried his level best to help Dustin but when the pistol used had only his fingerprints on it, he gave up the last hope. The body of the only witness who had agreed to give testimony was found two kilometres away from Travis Springs in a car crash site. There was no proof of a possibility of a murder. Drunken driving was the cause of death.

Dustin was sentenced to 15 years of imprisonment for a murder he did not commit. He was devastated. All he had with him was the notebook of Jade. He requested the authorities for permission for keeping it with him. His granny saw him at prison and cried every time she visited him. Jade wasn't allowed as she was a minor.

He cried like a man who had lost everything in life. All his dreams and aspirations were finished. He would never be able to lead a normal life again. He was very concerned about his granny. Without him, she wouldn't be able to run the restaurant. They had no other relative to whom she could ask for help.

Jade heard the news of Dustin's imprisonment and her reason to live ended there and then. She lost consciousness out of shock. Her father and siblings admitted her to the hospital for emergency treatment. The shock was too much for her brain to process. She was into a state of psychological shock. For two weeks, she received treatment for emotional trauma.

After two weeks when she was released from the hospital, her dad sent her to Alabama to her maternal grandparents house. Jade was admitted to a school there and her life went on like an automaton's.

The wish to live was taken out of her very soul. She didn't talk much and waited for the day when she could complete her school and be an adult. Then she would visit Dustin everyday at the prison.

She would wait for him for 15 years and.then when he would be released, she would tell him how much she loved him. This thought provided her with some energy and she studied hard to complete her schooling.

Chapter Four

T wo years later

Two years passed by and Jade graduated from school. Her dad and siblings regularly visited her. No one was allowed to mention Dustin in fear that she would again land up in the hospital. She wanted to ask so many questions but everyone avoided the sore topic. It pained her to see that to them Dustin had just disappeared from the face of the earth. The last two years her dad did not allow her to visit Travis Springs.

She finally packed her bags and said goodbye to her home of two years. Hugging her grandparents for bearing up with her, she promised to visit them soon. Jaden had come to take her back home and she couldn't be happier. She was an adult now and could visit Dustin in the prison. She would go and check up with his granny.

The familiar faces and surroundings of Travis Springs calmed her soul. She felt like she was free again. Her dad welcomed her with open arms. Her dad looked happier and everyone informed that Jayson and her dad patched up. Jayson was in love and marrying the love of his life. She knew that her older brother Jayson and her dad had a fight long back and they were not on talking terms. Jayson had left home. So the news of their patching up was a welcome surprise to the whole family.

Her father had invited Jayson and his fiancée to dinner in the evening. She waited eagerly to meet her oldest brother, who was thirteen years older to her. Juliette hugged her too. She was studying architecture in Austin. Jade caught up with the latest gossip happening in their lives. She missed home so much.

In the evening, Jade met Jayson and Karen. They made wedding plans and bonded after a long time.

Two days later, Jade went to Dustin's restaurant to visit his granny. The restaurant looked the same as it did two years earlier.

Opening the door, she was surprised to see a solitary customer sitting although it was lunchtime. At this time, usually the place would be full of customers. She saw the empty seat at the cash counter. Dustin would sit there and stare at her. Where was granny?

She went inside the kitchen and saw a very frail looking granny, cooking for the man. Only a single attendant was there to help her. Her heart broke at the sight.

"Granny?" She squeaked, her voice was choked with suppressed tears and refused to cooperate.

Granny turned around and saw her. She froze as if she had seen a ghost.

"Jade?" She whispered in disbelief.

"Yes granny, you remember me?" She asked, with tears in her eyes.

"Oh sweetheart, you came? How can I forget you? I thought you forgot. It's been two years," said granny.

The attendant went out to serve the customer his order.

"Dad sent me away to Alabama, granny. I wasn't allowed to come back. Now I'm 18. I'm an adult. No one can stop me. How's Dustin, granny?" She asked, hesitantly.

Her granny sighed deeply. "He's broken. He has lost the reason to live. He doesn't talk whenever I go to see him," said granny, wiping the tears in her eyes.

"I'm eighteen now. I want to go and see him granny. Can you tell me the prison and cell details?" She asked and granny wrote down all the details on a piece of paper.

Jade helped in the restaurant a little, "Why aren't there any customers, granny?" She asked, confusedly. Ever since she arrived, there were only two solitary customers.

"Ever since Dustin was sent to prison, the people of Travis Springs do not come here anymore, " granny said, with a heavy heart and a painful expression.

"But why? We have to do something to bring them back, " said Jade.

"What can we do?" Asked granny helplessly.

"Let me think, granny. I'll come up with something," she said with hope. She had to do something to keep Dustin's dream restaurant up and running.

Jade took her leave promising to return soon. The next whole week she was busy with college admissions. She wanted to study Bachelor of business administration - marketing from University of Austin. She wanted to handle Dustin's restaurant and make it so successful that when Dustin was released from prison, he would be happy.

She easily got admission and her classes started a week later. She didn't want to relocate to Austin. It was just a 25 minute drive away and she drove to college everyday and back. She had to help granny at the restaurant. She couldn't still think.of something to improve the sales at Dustin's restaurant.

It was a Saturday and she did not have college. She drove to Imperial prison to see Dustin. Her heart sang and she was excited at the prospect of seeing him. Her love for him had increased over the years. She parked her car and got down and went straight to the gates. Showing her identity card, she went inside, spoke to the prison guards and waited for Dustin.

She couldn't contain her excitement. It had been 2 long years since she had seen him last. The wait seemed to stretch forever. The guard returned alone. She searched beside him, behind him to see if Dustin was following him, but no. There was no Dustin.

"Sorry ma'am. The prisoner does not know you. He has refused to meet you," he said, with a sorry smile on his face.

Jade stood shocked at what he told her. Dustin didn't recognise her? How could he forget her so soon? Two years, only two years was enough to forget her? He didn't want to see her?

Tears streamed down her cheeks. "There must be a mistake, sir. I'm Jade Meyers. Did you inform Dustin Moore that I have come to see him?" She implored.

"Yes miss. I told him exactly that. He doesn't know you and he doesn't wish to see you. I'm sorry, I can't do anything else," he said apologetically.

Jade went back the way she came. Her eyes were full of tears. She felt devastated. For two years she faced life with only one hope. When she would grow up and be able to see Dustin.

She returned home and locked the door of her room and sobbed her heart out. Her eyes were swollen and there were no tears left to fall.

She couldn't face the reality that Dustin didn't remember her anymore. She swore to herself that she would visit him every Saturday till he acknowledged her presence and came to meet her.

She didn't go to his restaurant for a week. She was too upset to face granny's questions. Life went on and classes went on. The next two weeks she went every Saturday to Imperial prisons with the hope of meeting Dustin. But she only faced disappointment every time. Dustin didn't want to meet her. He sent the same response through the prison guards. That didn't deter Jade even 1%. She was determined to make him remember her.

She visited granny and told her what happened. Granny was stunned by her grandson's reactions. She tried to comfort an upset Jade, but couldn't. Jade sobbed uncontrollably onto her frail shoulders. Her heart broke at the sight and she decided to talk to her grandson on her next visit.

Chapter Five

Jayson and Karen's wedding was coming up and Jade was a little busy with the preparations as the reception was to be held in the backyard of their house. She coordinated with the wedding planner and helped with the arrangements.

After the wedding was over, Juliette was abducted by her long time admirer Xavion. She was worried about them and didn't get much time to do anything else. A week later however, their dad relaxed after hearing the news of Juliette's engagement to Xavion. They planned to get married next week. So, again she and her dad got busy with their wedding preparations.

A week later, after Juliette and Xavion's wedding, life became normal. Jaden was in his final year of studies in Austin. He was planning to become a CPA.

Jade went to college everyday and went to help at granny's restaurant in the evenings. They had started special cookery workshops in the afternoons to teach special dishes and delicacies at nominal prices. The concept was Jade's and she printed out simple posters and promoted them by giving them to friends and acquaintances.

Soon these workshops became popular as women and girls flocked to learn. Money poured in and Jade spoke to them casually about how Dustin was framed. Everyone sympathised. It was a clever ploy to clear Dustin's name.

The women went home and spoke to their family members. Slowly the bar started filling in with men who wanted a good drink. Granny called back some of her old employees.

Jade went to meet Dustin every Saturday, religiously. She hoped one day he would meet her. But disappointment was a small word for what she felt when the guard returned with the same response. He felt ashamed of himself for giving her the heartbreaking news every time.

Granny tried to convince Dustin to talk to Jade once, for everything that she'd been doing for them. He didn't listen.

"No, granny. I can't. She's young and has a life ahead of her. I want her to move on and get married to a good guy. I want her to have a happily married life. I don't want her to wait for me for 15 years, granny. Please, let her go. Let her live her life. I beg of you," he said and went back to his cell.

His heart broke every time he had to say those words. Every Saturday he waited for her to come. He cried brokenly in his cell all on his own, with only Jade's notebook to keep him company. He didn't wish to give her hope. He didn't wish to waste away her life waiting for him. He couldn't be so selfish. He knew he was breaking her heart but that was the only way.

Jade however didn't give up hope. She went every Saturday to see him. When his granny requested him a lot, Dustin gave in. He decided to end it all and make her come to her senses and go ahead with her life.

So the next Saturday when she went and waited, the guard came grinning with Dustin following behind him. His hair was grown and he looked tired and haggard. He had an overgrown beard and melancholy, sad, sunken eyes. He wore a prisoner's uniform, covering his body. Gone were the biceps that she had touched the first day that she had met him.

Big fat tears fell from her eyes at the sight of him, "Dustin," she whispered, and the sob that she was choking on, broke out. She went forward to hug him to herself but he just held out his hand, gesturing at her to stop.

She stared at him in confusion. "Look, I don't want you to come here and make a fool of yourself. Leave me and my family alone. Will you? We don't need your pity. We can look after ourselves. I was just playing with you. All that's done, finished. Why can't you get it in your head? Are you so desperate for a fu*k? Just get lost. I'm sure there are many boys of your age, ready and willing. Just leave," he said and walked away to his cell, breaking down completely.

Jade walked towards the main door and out of Imperial prison forever. Her white face was indication enough that she received another shock. The third shock in her eighteen years of life. Her first shock was the news of her mom's death, which toppled her world. The second was the news of Dustin's imprisonment which landed her at the hospital and now the harsh words that she never expected Dustin could say to her.

She went back home and stayed in her room. She didn't cry, her eyes were dry. She didn't eat, she didn't talk.

When her dad found out after two days, he admitted her to the hospital again. Granny came to know about Jade's condition and had a word with her grandson.

Dustin felt very heartbroken for having said all those things to her, but when he heard that she was hospitalised because of him, he was devastated. He still waited for her every Saturday and when she didn't turn up, he didn't know whether to be happy or sad. Truth was he wanted her to come for him. He wanted her to wait for him. He wanted her to love him. He wanted to be selfish but he knew he couldn't. He had to let her go and that was the only possible way. His granny tried to make him understand that Jade truly loved him but he tried to discourage her. Jade was the daughter of the richest man in Travis Springs and had a bright future ahead of her. Forgetting him would do her good. He had nothing to offer her.

After a week, Jade was released from the hospital and sent to Austin to stay with Jaden and complete her studies. She concentrated on her studies and came home only to see her dad.

She didn't go to meet granny or Dustin after that day. She didn't talk much to anyone. She just carried on with her life.

She studied hard and stayed home to cook or to read. She didn't have any friends and didn't go out even when Jaden forced her to. Jaden was concerned but there was no way he could help her.

So life continued and studies continued for the next two years.

Chapter Six

T wo years later

The news of her dad's ill health, brought Jade home. She didn't wish to return to Austin and leave her dad alone. So she drove to college and back everyday.

Jaden was living in Travis Springs with his girlfriend whom he loved and they were expecting their first child together. Her dad invited all her siblings and their families to dinner.

She liked Jaden's girlfriend, Rosalie. She was a very sweet and kindhearted woman and they bonded well although she was 5 years older than Jade.

Throughout dinner she felt the vacuum in her life seeing her siblings happily settled with their life partners. Jayson had twins, and Juliette had a baby boy while Jaden's girlfriend was expecting. She loved them all and watched them interact with each other. She wasn't the eloquent and bold type who could chat non-stop and pour out all her personal problems to anyone and everyone. So she quietly noticed everything and smiled, although the smile never reached her eyes.

After dinner everyone took their leave and Jade escorted a pregnant Rosalie to her car. Jaden was talking to their dad and would join them in a minute.

Rosalie held Jade's hand and said,"See you soon, Jade. We will be happy if you come down to our house sometimes."

"Yeah, I will. You will then soon get tired of me. I don't have many places to goto actually, " said Jade.

"Why? A pretty girl like you didn't have places to goto? Don't you have a boyfriend?" asked Rosalie.

Jade let out a deep sigh. For the first time in her life she wanted to talk to someone about Dustin, "I love someone for the last four years of my life but he doesn't love me back," she said dejectedly.

"You could win him over, " Rosalie suggested.

"No I can't. He's not around. I can't see him," she said, staring at some far away object, unfocused.

"Why? What happened to him?" Asked Rosalie, scared that he might not be alive maybe.

"He's in prison. He had been falsely convicted of murder and sentenced to 15 years in prison," she said and Rosalie's jaw dropped at the tragic news.

"You could meet him at the prison, " suggested Rosalie.

"He wouldn't meet me. He says he doesn't recognise me," she said as large teardrops fell from her eyes.

Rosalie hugged her tightly. "Why didn't you ask for Jayson's help?" She asked.

"My family doesn't want me to mention his name. No one's interested. They behave as if Dustin never existed," she told her, wiping her tears.

"I could talk to Jaden and have his case reopened," Rosalie suggested and Jade's eyes shone with new found hope.

"You think it could happen? I'll be forever indebted to you Rosalie," she said, holding her hands.

"Please sweetie, you're just like my own sister. I'll talk to Jaden and inform you. Ok?" She said and Jade nodded.

Jaden came rushing out of the house and they left to go home.

The next day, Rosalie thought about how to approach Jaden and convince him to take up the case of the man whom Jade loved. She realised that she had forgotten to ask his name and details. Without knowing anything about him, she couldn't convince Jaden.

In the afternoon, Jade visited Rosalie on her way back from college.

"Have lunch with me, Jade?" Rosalie asked.

"Sure, thanks," said Jade. They sat down at the table and Betty, Rosalie's housekeeper served them lunch.

"Did you tell bro?" Asked Jade, hopefully.

"I will tonight but you need to give me some details about him," she told Jade.

"His name's Dustin Moore. He used to run his restaurant 'Jenny's Restaurant and Bar' at the marketplace here in Travis Springs. His grandma Jenny helped him run it. They are honest, hard working people Rosalie. He's as old as Jaden. They were classmates in school. Dustin's parents died and he dropped out. He and his grandma started this restaurant at their home," Jade told her.

"Oh. What happened to him? How he was convicted of murder?" Asked Rosalie.

"Four drunken men had come over to his bar. They started a brawl amongst themselves. It was a nasty fight. One of them had a pistol. Dustin tried to separate them. One with the pistol fired a shot at his friend who died on the spot. Before Dustin could react, the actual murderer placed the gun in Dustin's hands and escaped the scene. The police arrested Dustin. The man who actually did it had political connections and escaped," said Jade, unhappily.

"Ok, I will talk to Jaden tonight. Don't worry," Rosalie promised.

They ate lunch and talked about Jaden's dad's health and Jade's studies. Jade left after lunch.

In the evening, Jaden came home and had dinner. After dinner, they went up to their bedroom.

"Jaden, do you know Dustin moore?" Rosalie asked him.

He looked at her with a vague expression. "Yeah, he was my classmate. He used to run a restaurant at the marketplace. He murdered a man and is rotting in jail," he said with a blank face.

"He didn't murder the man. How can you conclude? Did you witness the murder?" Asked Rosalie.

"Why are you supporting his case so much? Don't tell me that you have fallen in love with him," he said, frowning.

"Don't be ridiculous. It's not me, Jade loves him," she said.

"It's nothing serious, just a crush. Dustin is a criminal and Jade should get over him," he said, turning his face towards his mobile with frustration.

"Jaden, how can you say so? For 4 long years she's loved the guy. Didn't you ever notice the sadness in her soul? What if Jennifer murdered Mr McAllister and convicted me? What if I would have been in jail for 15 years on false charges? Would you forget me?" Said Rosalie. Jennifer was Rosalie's stepmother who had forced Rosalie to marry her acquaintance, Mr Allen McAllister. Jaden saved her from the marriage.

"Never, I would knock every possible option and get you released," said Jaden with a fierce conviction.

"Then do so for Dustin too, please. Do you think Jade will love and marry another in this lifetime? All you siblings are happy and settled. Don't you want the same for your little sister? Don't you want her to be happily settled with the love of her life?" Said Rosalie, with tears in her eyes. Why couldn't Jaden see how important this was for Jade?

"Don't cry love. Of course I want Jade to be happy. If her happiness lies with Dustin, then I'll see what I can do about it. Don't stress yourself please. It's not good for you and our baby," said Jaden with concern written all over his face.

"Tell Jayson to take up his case, please," said Rosalie.

"I'll first have the incident investigated and then approach Jayson with evidence and facts. But it will take time as the incident occurred 4 years back," he told her.

"Thank you Jaden. At least we can try," she said, snuggling into him. "I can't imagine what I would have done had I been in Jade's place. I would have died without you Jaden. I must say that Jade is very strong," she said.

"I didn't know. She never told me, she loves him. I'm so happy that she trusted you enough to talk about her problems with you. We all know she's depressed but didn't know why," he said.

Chapter Seven

The next day Jaden went to his dad's law firm where he was working as a CPA. He called his Private Investigator, Robert Harrison, who had helped him find Rosalie. He asked him to investigate exactly what happened at Dustin Moore's bar cum restaurant the night of the murder and collect as much evidence as he could.

After a few days Jade was busy with Rosalie and Jaden's wedding. Her life continued as before, with college and home, home and college. She went to spend some time with her nephew and niece at Jayson's house or with Juliette's son after college.

Three months passed by and yet the PI, whom her brother hired could not produce any results. Jade finally took his number from Rosalie and called him.

He came to meet her at a small cafe outside her college. "Hello, Mr Harrison, I'm Jade Meyers, Jaden's sister," she introduced herself.

"Hello ma'am, pleased to meet you. Tell me why you summoned me?" He asked courteously.

"Mr Harrison, I want to know what you found out about Dustin Moore's case," she asked directly without further ado.

"I couldn't find much ma'am. No one seems to have seen the men who had come to the bar that night," he said.

"I've seen them. I have witnessed the murder Mr Harrison. I was there at the restaurant at that time and I could tell you about three people who were there too and witnessed the murder. One of them wanted to give testimony against the actual culprit but he was murdered too. His body was found 2 miles away at a car crash site. The police gave the verdict of drunken driving," she said and Mr Harrison listened to her intently.

"I don't want you to give any testimony ma'am. It's very risky. But yes, I want your help in making a rough sketch of the people whom you saw. Can you help me with that? I have tried to locate the ex employees of the restaurant but couldn't. It seems everyone is scared to open their mouths," said Mr Harrison.

"Yeah, the man is very influential. I could help you sketch him and three of his accomplices. I could also help you make a sketch of the other two people who were there at the restaurant at that time," she said.

Mr Harrison pulled out his notebook from his backpack. "Yes that would be very helpful ma'am. First we will draw the culprit," he said, excitedly. They spent the next half an hour drawing the culprit. Once the sketch was ready and both were happy with the outcome, he drew his accomplices too. After two hours, they left the coffee shop. Jade had to return home else her dad would get worried about her. They planned to meet again the next day, at the same time in this very coffee shop.

Jade went home happily. Finally something productive was happening. Finally she was able to do something for Dustin and his granny. She thought hard how she could help in the investigation.

The next day again she met Mr Harrison and they drew sketches of the two other customers who witnessed the murder. "You could meet Richardson who was a past employee of the restaurant. He was granny's right hand and he too witnessed everything. Promise them anonymity and they might give important information, Mr Harrison," said Jade.

"Yes ma'am. Thank you so much for helping me. Mr Meyers has been at my throat for the last three months for not producing any results," he said, gratefully.

"I also want you to do another thing Mr Harrison. The fingerprint report might be sabotaged as the culprit wasn't wearing any gloves. So his fingerprints should have been there, but the report that was submitted to the police had only Dustin's fingerprints. Could you get hold of the actual reports if they haven't been destroyed yet?" She asked.

"Yes ma'am, I will and then update you. You have my number, if you remember anything else, please call me," he said. They left the cafe.

Jade waited patiently everyday for his call only he didn't call. One month flew by and still no result. Her patience had worn out and she ultimately called him.

"Mr Harrison, Jade Meyers here. You didn't revert back?"she asked him.

"I will ma'am. It's a very complicated case. Every lead only gives me disappointment. Richardson's family vanished the day after he left his job at the restaurant. Of the two witnesses, one is dead and the other is missing. The rest of the ex employees wouldn't open their mouths. The officer who had taken out the fingerprint report has been transferred. I'm now tracking him down. Mr Meyers had a word with the sheriff, Chase McGuire. He's a friend of your older brother, Jayson Meyers. Mr McGuire is helping in the case too," he said.

"Ok Mr Harrison. Please do keep me updated, " she said, dejectedly.

The next nine months, they kept hunting for evidence, yet couldn't get anything worthwhile. Jade was disappointed. There had to be a way to prove Dustin innocent.

When she felt totally hopeless, she thought of granny. Maybe she could help in some way. She drove to the marketplace and parked in front of the restaurant. The place was locked? Didn't granny live here anymore? She had never seen the restaurant locked. She went to the backside and knocked on the door of Dustin's apartment. It looked very dirty from outside as if no one lived here anymore. Maybe granny had left and gone to some relatives house.

She rang the bell, yet no one opened the door. After repeatedly ringing nearly five times, she gave up hope and turned to go away when the door slowly creaked open.

She turned around, her eyes widened at the sight of granny. Pale, thin, hardly able to stand on her feet. Granny was about to fall down but Jade ran up to her and caught her just on time.

"Granny, what happened to you?" She sobbed.

"You've come, my child?" Granny said feebly.

"Yes, granny, I'll never leave you again. Tell me what happened to you?" She said, helping granny to her room and laying her on the bed.

"I'm fine dear, " she said, feebly.

Jade called her family doctor urgently. "Did you eat anything granny?" She asked her.

"No, sweetheart. I can't cook," she said.

"I'll make something for you," she said. She rushed to the kitchen and saw that there was nothing in the house to cook.

She returned back to granny's room. "There's nothing to cook. I've got money, but I couldn't go to buy anything. A well wisher had been regularly sending me money, but I couldn't get up and go to the shop," she said.

"Let the doctor check you first. Then I'll get the things for you along with your medicines. Ok?" Jade said.

"I don't need a doctor, dear," said granny.

"Don't you want to be fit and open the restaurant again? Don't you want to be healthy and wait for Dustin's release?" She scolded.

"Yes I do want. But I couldn't save the restaurant. After you left, everyone stopped coming too," she said.

"I'm sorry granny. We will think of a way to pull it up again. But first let's get you better," said Jade.

Chapter Eight

The doctor came and checked granny. It wasn't anything serious. She was weak and dehydrated. She was very anaemic and her bones had become brittle. The doctor prescribed some medicines to improve her bone health and also medicines to improve her haemoglobin levels.

"Make her eat home cooked nourishing meals, and she would be fit as before," said the doctor.

After he left, Jade went to buy some food items and necessities for granny. She returned and made some chicken soup and fed granny with bread. She gave her medicines.

"There's more soup in the kitchen, granny. If you're hungry, there's milk and cereal too," said Jade.

"I'm feeling better already. You go, I will eat that if I'm hungry. I'll sleep now," she said.

"Ok, I'll come in the evening and cook dinner for you. Ok?" Said Jade and granny nodded.

Jade kissed granny and left. She wanted to tell granny that they were trying to reopen Dustin's case but decided against it. Without substantial proof there was no surety that they could reopen the case. She went home and got ready for her extra class at college.

After college, she again went to make dinner for granny. She made her a stew and rice and fed her.

"Drink a glass of warm milk before you sleep, ok?" She instructed granny.

"Yes dear, I will, thank you. Will you switch on the TV, please?" Her granny asked.

She switched on the TV and handing out the remote control to granny, she left to go home.

After seven months, she received a call from Harrison. "Ma'am, we've located the culprit at a small village in Louisiana. His name's Johnny Brownhill. Used to work as a bodyguard of a local political leader but now because of a few drunken mishaps, he's been out of job for the last one year. So he has lost his political backing now. Our men are shadowing him. The moment we get some evidence we will nab him," said Harrison.

"Good. What about the officer who duplicated the reports?" Asked Jade.

"We've found him. He has owned up and willing to help only if we don't hand him over to the higher authorities," said Mr Harrison.

"That's good news. So have you started searching?" She asked.

"Yeah, he's coordinating with sheriff Chase McGuire and they're hunting everywhere for it," said Mr Harrison. "Also your brother Jayson Meyers has taken an interest in the case. He's thinking of how to get more evidence. Now it's a matter of a few months. We will get evidence and open up the case," he said.

Jade was happy with the latest developments in the case. She was sure that with Jayson now taking an interest in it, things would speed up. It still wasn't time to inform granny. She wanted some evidence to crop up and then she would surely inform granny.

The next two months, Jade dedicatedly looked after granny and bought her medicines. She had started her internship at a boutique in the marketplace where Karen's friend Valentina worked too. It wasn't far from granny's restaurant and she was happy. Before classes in the morning she cooked for granny and in the afternoon after returning from college, she went home, freshened up, had lunch and then went to work. After her working shift, she cooked for granny, ensured that she was fine and then returned home.

When granny started feeling a lot better, she started cooking again. It was her passion and she was happy to be able to cook again. In two more weeks granny was back to her form.

"Granny let's open the restaurant again," said Jade and granny agreed. She called in one of her old employees to get the restaurant and it's kitchen cleaned.

After a week's cleaning, they could again open the restaurant. Granny was very excited and she called back her cook too.

A few customers came in curious as to why the restaurant was closed for so long. They had coffee and cakes with granny and talked to her. They demanded the workshops that Jade and granny used to conduct. So, again the workshops started like before and money poured in. Granny was very happy and so was Jade.

After a month, Mr Harrison called her to update her, "Yes, Mr Harrison, tell me what news you have to give me," said Jade.

"Ma'am the original fingerprint report has been found and the sheriff has arrested Johnny Brownhill. He's under police custody but hasn't yet accepted his crime. Your brother, Jayson Meyers has applied for a reopening of Dustin's case. As soon as the court accepted his petition, he would start pleading innocent on Dustin's behalf, " said Mr Harrison.

"Thank you Mr Harrison, that's the best news I've heard so far," said Jade with a smile on her lips.

"There's more. Your brother had also announced a cash reward for anyone who could provide us evidence. The money is huge, and the person's anonymity would be kept intact, so I think we will get to collect more evidence now, "said Mr Harrison.

"Yeah, I think so too. Do keep me updated Mr Harrison, " she said. He disconnected the call and Jade happily went to work. In the evening she would tell granny.

She couldn't concentrate much on her work. She started thinking about Dustin's release and how granny would react. Would Dustin be happy to see her?

Then she remembered what he said to her and all her enthusiasm to meet him went away. No, he wouldn't be happy to see her. Who was she? Just a simple girl who crushed on him? Who he was just playing with? Who thought it to be the real thing and fell for him instead?

She sighed and went to granny's house after work. She told granny everything that had been going on since that talk with Rosalie. Granny was ecstatic,"Do you think they really would release him?" She asked Jade as tears of happiness fell from her eyes. She couldn't contain her happiness. Tomorrow she'd be visiting Dustin. She would have to tell him what Jade had done for him in spite of his cruel words to her.

"Yes granny, Jayson's announced a huge cash prize for anyone who could provide evidence," said Jade.

"But I have no money to pay him," said granny, worried.

"You don't need to pay granny. Jayson's loaded. He'll pay. He gets so involved in his cases that he would do anything to give justice to those who need it," said Jade.

"But why would he spend so much?" Said granny.

"Because of my happiness," she said shyly and granny grinned and hugged her to her bosom.

"I might have done something very good that I now have you, sweetheart. You're a godsend to me," she said and kissed Jade's forehead.

"I love you, granny," said Jade

"I love you too, sweetheart," said granny.

A whole whole month went by and the restaurant was picking up. The news of the arrest of Johnny Brownhill brought more customers to the restaurant. The case reopening created quite a stir in Travis Springs and those who were against the Moore family too started changing their judgements. The bar sales picked up.

All the old employees returned. Richardson too heard about the arrest and came back from Virginia, where he was hiding with his family. Johnny Brownhill had threatened to murder his two children if he stayed at Travis Springs and opened his mouth, so he had escaped.

So, everything was going well and everyone was eagerly waiting for the court to accept Jayson's petition.

Chapter Nine

The court didn't accept the petition due to lack of evidence. They wanted more evidence to open up the case. Everyone was disappointed. Jayson put on his thinking cap, trying to think of a way to get more evidence. It would only be possible if someone opened their mouth.

Jade and granny were very depressed after the court's rejection. Granny didn't have the heart to tell Dustin anything. So life went on till some miracle would occur and the case could be reopened.

After six months, the police arrested the two other accomplices of Johnny Brownhill. One of them was hiding in Chicago while the other was in New Jersey. Their arrest brought a fresh spurt of energy to the case. Jayson announced a hefty sum of money to whoever provided them proof. However this time he gave a month's time to come up with the proof else the offer would stand null and void.

This gave Jade hope that maybe someone would come up with some evidence. They all waited and waited. Jade went to visit Jaden and Rosalie's twins regularly to play with them.

The Meyers family still continued their monthly family get together to bond with everyone. Jade's college was over and she could now only concentrate on her internship. It gave her a lot of free time to help granny at her restaurant.

After twenty-seven days, Jayson got a call from an unknown number.

"Hello, I can send you evidence but I have some conditions," said a male, hoarse voice.

"What conditions?" Asked Jayson.

"You have to delete my number the moment you receive the video. You cannot mention my number to anyone. Also you have to pay me by cash," said the man.

"Ok, done. Only if the video you send is genuine and not fake and if it helps in the case," said Jayson.

"I will send someone to your house to pick up the cash at 7 o'clock in the evening. No questions asked. He will say a password that I will send you with the video," he said.

"Sure," said Jayson.

"Ok," said the man.

He disconnected the call and Jayson waited impatiently for the video that the man wanted to send. Sure enough, after 15 long minutes, his phone vibrated with a message.

He checked to see that a video and the password had been sent. Downloading the video, he started to watch it. His eyes went wide with surprise and he sat down to support his legs.

It was the entire recording of the events that took place that evening, the night of the murder. It started with a drunken brawl which after sometime Dustin tried to stop and then the murder where it was clearly visible that

Johnny Brownhill pulled the trigger to kill the man and then placed the pistol in Dustin's hands and shooting the CCTV camera, left the crime scene.

Jayson Meyers had a spring in his step. He had the evidence that he had been wanting for so long. He picked up Jaden from his house and rushed to the sheriff's office and showed him the footage.

They showed the footage to Johnny Brownhill and he broke down completely. He owned up to his crime and Chase McGuire recorded it.

With all these evidence, Jayson filed a fresh petition for Dustin's case to be reopened. He, Jaden and Chase went to Imperial prisons to inform Dustin about his case.

Dustin sat with his eyes wide open at the news that his case would be reopened. He never in his best dreams thought it would be possible. He pinched himself again and again to see if he was dreaming. He didn't know why Jayson and Jaden were taking so much interest in his case. Did it have something to do with Jade? No, it couldn't. Jade had forgotten him and maybe moved on with her life.

His granny never mentioned Jade in her talks. She had stopped coming for months and then suddenly a few months back, came to meet him. She was looking happy and energetic. Dustin also didn't talk much. He wanted to know about Jade but didn't know how to ask his granny.

"I can't pay your fees, Mr Meyers," he told him, with his eyes cast downwards.

"I don't need you to pay me anything,mesaid Jayson with a smile. "I'm just helping out since you're innocent. I want you to get justice," said Jayson.

"Thank you so much, I don't know how to thank you all," he said with his eyes sparkling with tears of happiness.

"We're just doing our job," said Chase, patting his back and he went out to have a talk with the prison warden. Jayson went too.

Jaden patted Dustin and said,"Thank Jade, bro. It's because of her love for you that I initiated the investigation. It's only for her happiness that Jayson has taken up your case," said Jaden and Dustin's jaw dropped and he stared at Jaden without a blink of his eye. Jade still loved him despite what he said to her? She hadn't moved on? How did he get so lucky?

"If I would have been you, I would have started working out to rebuild my biceps and six-pack. Do you want Jade to see you this way?" Said Jaden, winking at him and leaving.

Dustin went back to his cell and kept thinking about what Jaden told him. He tried his best to make her move on and forget him. But she didn't. She really loved him. He grinned happily at the thought, sighing heavily and waiting to apologise to her. He couldn't sleep the whole night with excitement. He held her notebook to his heart and kissed it again and again.

"Oh my Jade, I wish you were in my arms right now," he thought aloud.

Then he looked at his frail body. No, he couldn't let Jade see him like this. He would again get back in shape for her.

In the evening, a man with a mask over his head, came to Jayson's house and said the password. Jayson handed him the cash and he went away. From the way he walked, Jayson Meyers knew who the man was who sent him the video. He himself had come to collect the cash as they had the same hoarse voice. Richardson, Dustin's grandma's trusted employee.

Jayson as promised didn't utter a word to anyone to protect the anonymity of Richardson. He was thankful that at least Richardson had the courage to save his employer. He had the presence of mind to record what happened that night.

So everyone waited for the court's decision with lots of eagerness. Dustin worked out for Jade while Jade helped granny at the restaurant and also managed her job. She waited eagerly for Dustin's release, hoping everyday that the court would give it's approval.

Chapter Ten

They waited and waited for the court's approval but in vain. Just like all legal systems take ages to respond, this was no different. Jayson repeatedly sent reminders yet the court seemed to take ages. Dustin was frustrated, Jade was impatient, Jaden lost hope, Jayson was relentless in his efforts but granny went about her work with a happy smile on her crinkled face.

"How are you not getting frustrated, granny?" Asked Jade.

"Courts have millions of pending cases. They will prioritise and set dates. It might take years or maybe just a few months if we're lucky. We have to be patient, dear," she explained.

Jade took a deep breath and tried to be as patient as possible.

At last after five long months, the court accepted the petition and gave permission to reopen the case. The date set for the hearing was after three more months.

They waited patiently for the hearing. Jayson was prepared and so was Chase.

Finally the day arrived and granny too went to the court along with many people of Travis Springs. Jade didn't have the courage to face Dustin. She stayed in her room and prayed. The whole day she couldn't eat a morsel of food. She was so nervous. She just sat down on her bed and just prayed.

By afternoon when Jaden called her, she trembled like a leaf, waiting for the news she had dreamt to hear for the last eight years.

"Jade, we've won the case. We've freed your Dustin. Jayson has applied for compensation from the state government on charges of false imprisonment and defamation. So Dustin would receive a lot of money as compensation. Now are you happy, Jade?" He asked softly.

Jade couldn't answer. Her voice was choked with tears of relief. Yes she was happy. The happiest she had ever been in the last eight years. "Yes, thanks Jady," she said and Jaden smiled.

"Today Dustin will be released and allowed to go home," he informed.

"Hmm," said Jade.

"See you later, bye, take care," said Jaden.

"You too," she answered. He hung up and Jade sat, unable to move. For years she had waited for this day and when it finally came, she was unable to go to granny's house and meet her Dustin. Her Dustin? No he wasn't hers.

She stayed at home fidgeting around in her room. Her mind was on what Dustin would be doing at home. He surely had arrived and was spending precious moments with his granny. She didn't have the courage to face him. What would she say? Hey, I've come to see you? How have you been? No. It's better to say nothing and stay at home.

Dustin came home at last after eight long years. His home and restaurant was just like he had left them. It was a miracle. He never expected that he would find things running so smoothly after he returned. His granny hugged him and cried with happiness.

She thought Jade would come to meet them but strangely she didn't. She found out from the boutique that she didn't come to work also. Dustin searched for Jade, thinking that she would be there to greet him, but when he realised that Jade wasn't coming to see him, he was very disappointed.

His granny told him everything that she had done for her and the restaurant. His wish to see her grew all the more. The next morning, he would search her out and meet her surely. He took a fresh shower and had his granny's dinner and went to bed, his cosy bed, his own room.

The next morning, he woke up early and showered and opened his restaurant with a new hope. It was a new beginning for him. He was free again. Granny too prepared the kitchen. Their employees came to work. Some of the people of Travis Springs came to greet him. They had coffee and chatted with him.

Afterwards the breakfast crowd came by and they got busy. Dustin managed the cash counters as before while granny handled the kitchen. Everytime the small bell on the door jingled to indicate someone's presence, he looked up, expecting Jade, only to find a customer in her place.

At last at 10:30 in the morning, Jade opened the restaurant door and came in. She slowly turned around and saw Dustin at the cash counter. Dustin stopped what he was doing and simply stared at her. She had grown so beautiful. She had bloomed into a woman of twenty-four. Her body had filled up so well. She had become taller and more curvy. Her eyelashes grew longer and her hair had grown too. Her complexion looked soft and creamy.

He wanted to get up and just take her in his arms and crush her to himself and kiss her like there was no tomorrow but with customers in the restaurant, he couldn't. So he just kept sitting there and staring at her with his jaws dropped.

Jade saw him, smiled shyly and went to the kitchen without a word. Was she ignoring him? Did she not feel happy to see him? He sat there, wanting to go to the kitchen and talk to her. Jade helped granny in the kitchen like always. For two hours she didn't come out. Dustin grew more and more impatient. When only one customer was left, he asked Richardson to sit at the cash counter and went inside to check what Jade was upto in the kitchen. He opened the door and stood watching Jade help granny make preparations for the dishes on the menu.

"Go and talk to your Dustin, dear," said granny with a smile.

"He's not mine," she said, pouting. Dustin's eyebrows went up in surprise at their topic of discussion.

"By the way, he now looks like a grumpy old man with so much beard," said Jade, chuckling.

Granny laughed. "That's true. I hate beards too," she agreed.

"So do I, eww," said Jade and continued with her chopping.

"I heard that," said Dustin in his deep husky voice. Both women whirled around and saw him. Granny chuckled and shook her head while Jade turned red as a tomato. She could feel Dustin's gaze on her and she kept chopping to just complete her work and escape from this place.

"So you have nothing to do than discuss me?" He asked.

Before Jade could say anything, granny said, "Don't say anything to her. She has a job to do after this yet she comes daily to help me. She won't come in your way Dustin. She'll just help me and go away, " said granny. Dustin just stared at granny. He wouldn't have said anything to Jade. He just wanted to hold her in his arms and kiss her senseless.

Jade completed her work. "Granny, I'm done for today, I'll go now," she said and opened the door of the kitchen and walked out. She went to her boutique to start her work.

Dustin felt frustrated as ever. He wanted to talk to her but he couldn't. She was gone for the day and he only had to wait for tomorrow to see her.

Chapter Eleven

J ade couldn't concentrate on anything throughout the day. She heaved a sigh of relief when her duty was over and she was free to go home. She thought of going to the restaurant to see what Dustin was doing but didn't want to piss him off by going there repeatedly. So she dragged herself home and had dinner and went to bed.

The next morning, she had early duty at the boutique so she went to the restaurant at 8 o'clock in the morning. Dustin wasn't there at the cash counter. Richardson sat there and wished her a good morning. She went to the kitchen and found granny searching for something.

"What are you looking for, granny?" She asked.

"My can of olives which I had pitted and marinated," she said as a few customers came in.

"Oh, I'll look for it," she offered.

"I think I left it in the kitchen at home. Here, take the keys and get them, will you please?" She said handing over the keys to her.

"Sure," she said, taking the keys and going at the backside to granny's kitchen.

She opened the apartment and went to the kitchen. She started looking at the cabinets. She forgot to ask where granny kept the olives. She searched the next cabinet, mumbling to herself where the olives could have escaped to.

"Are you looking for me?" Said the husky voice of Dustin from behind her.

She whirled around and came nose to nose with Dustin clad only in a towel. He must have just showered. She blushed seeing his muscular, toned bare body for the first time, that too so close to hers. A water droplet trickled from his hair to his chest and downwards. Dustin stared at her, noticing her checking him out. He looked at what she was watching and smirked seeing the water droplet.

She blushed and turned away. "No, I'm searching for granny's olives. She asked me to," she said. Her eyes suddenly fell upon the jar on the kitchen counter. Before she could pick it up, Dustin turned her around. "Don't you want to talk to me?" He asked her, noting her red cheeks and downcast eyes.

"I have nothing to say to you, " she said.

"Nothing at all? I shaved my beard. Won't you like to see me now?" He asked, holding her chin and making her look up.

She looked into his eyes and was lost. "Am I looking grumpy and old now?" He whispered, his arm going round her waist and pulling her flush onto his body.

She gasped as her body touched his hard chest. "I was just joking, " she mumbled, looking down, her hand going up to his chest to put some distance between themselves. He hissed at her touch, goosebumps appeared on his body where she touched him. She immediately removed her hands, but he placed them back on him, loving the feel of her soft hands on his bare body.

"I'm not joking. I'm waiting for my welcome home kiss," he said and her eyes widened in shock.

"I need to get the olives to granny," she said, with a flushed face.

"Give me my kiss and then go," he said, pulling her closer to him. She felt his arousal poking into her. He lowered his head and stared at her mouth longingly. Her hands went around his neck and she pulled his head close to her mouth, closing her eyes as she planted a small peck on his lower lip.

He was lost in the small gesture. His other hand held her head and his hungry mouth claimed her lips. It was a passionate kiss, fuelled by the thirst of their souls. A thirst that only could be quenched by the other. He had dreamt of kissing her every day for the last eight years. His tongue entered her mouth and tasted it's sweetness. His mouth trying to relive every dream that he had of kissing her. His kiss turned insatiable, demanding her to kiss him back. She kissed him back then sudden realisation hit her.

He was playing with her! He knew she loved him.

"No," she protested against his lips, her palms, flat on his chest, trying to break free. He released her, confused at her sudden change of mood.

"Don't play games with me, please," she said, with tears in her eyes. She picked up the can of olives and ran out of his apartment.

Dustin stood transfixed to the spot, hurt by her words. He remembered he had said these very words to her long back. The words affected her so much he had no idea. He had to comfort her, he had to apologise. He had to prove that he never played with her.

He loved her. He loved her with every pore in his body, with every breath that he took and with every beat of his heart.

He slowly got dressed and went to the restaurant to start his day. Jade was nowhere to be seen. He looked for her in the kitchen but she had left. He went back dejectedly to his cash counter. Another day had gone by and yet he was still unable to show her how much he loved her.

Jade couldn't stay at the restaurant and work with Dustin hovering around. She just couldn't forget the kiss. It stirred such feelings in her which she never experienced in her entire life. She was scared of these emotions as they made her vulnerable. She knew that what she felt for Dustin was for life. She could never love another so deeply. But she had her self respect too. She couldn't reduce herself to be his plaything. She won't be played with.

She overworked herself and returned home after a tiring day. The next whole week, she didn't go to the restaurant. They didn't need her anymore and she shouldn't let Dustin get the impression that she was around for something. She didn't want anything in return. She loved him so she had saved him. Same with granny. She loved granny so she saved her.

Jade worked at the boutique and then stayed home the rest of the time. She went to her brothers houses sometimes to play with the children.

After a miserable week, Jade walked slowly out of the boutique to her car. She missed Dustin very much, her eyes searched his restaurant from the outside for a glimpse of him. She stared towards his restaurant and then sighed heavily. Reaching her car, she was about to unlock it when she saw the flat tyre.

"Oh crap," she swore, kicking the tyre and muttering more swear words.

She would have to walk down at this hour. She stared at Dustin's restaurant thinking whether to ask Richardson for help when she heard Dustin's husky voice from behind her,"I can drop you, Jade," he said softly.

"No, thanks. I'll just ask Richardson, " she told him, walking towards the restaurant. She couldn't go far when Dustin caught her arm and spun her around.

"For God's sake Jade. Let me drop you home," he said, his hands falling helplessly to his sides.

"No, Dustin. I don't expect anything from you. I might love you but I'm not throwing myself at you. Please leave me alone," she said walking away to the restaurant to ask for Richardson's help. He again caught her wrist and pulled her close.

Dustin felt frustrated. He was at his wits end. Why couldn't she let him drop her home? "Look, I'm sorry. I'm really sorry that I said all those things to you. You know they're just to make you move on and marry a good guy and settle down. I care about you dammit. I didn't want you to wait for me for 15 years. I don't have anything to give you, Jade," he said, his hand touching her cheek tenderly. His eyes serious and solemn, longingly staring at her upturned face. "Please let me drop you home, Jade?"

"Ok," she said softly, closing her eyes at the feel of his tender touch on her cheek.

Chapter Twelve

He led her towards his motorcycle. He had it cleaned and lubricated and had gone for a test drive yesterday. It was still in perfect condition.

He handed her a helmet and fixed his own too. Then climbing onto his motorcycle, he sat waiting for her to sit. She climbed onto it behind his back, straddling the motorcycle. She sat keeping a good amount of distance between themselves when Dustin turned around and caught hold of her hand. He placed it around his torso, "Hold me," he insisted. When she kept her hold, he started his motorcycle and rode at a steady pace.

The wind swept through her hair and she felt carefree and happy. She could feel his rippling muscles beneath her palm, the heat seeping through his thin tee shirt onto her palm.

"Where are we going Dustin?" She asked, panicking to see that he had taken a detour from the path that led to her house.

"Just wait and watch," He answered, excitedly. He looked at her through the rearview mirror and grinned. What was he up to now?

They rode through a clear path that wound through grassy slopes with bluebonnets swaying in the evening breeze. The sun had set but the lights from either side of the road illuminated the area nicely. The moon seemed brighter than usual as it watched them from the clear sky.

"Are you kidnapping me?" She asked, looking around.

"It sounds like a good idea," he answered, chuckling. Jade loved his happy, infectious mood. It seemed like old times when they were younger. What she would give to see him this happy always. His mood caught on and she felt excited too.

After riding a little, Dustin led her to a clearing, where the sound of gurgling water caught her attention. Looking ahead, she saw a beautiful small brook of shallow clear water, illuminated by the motorcycle headlights.

She gasped at the beauty of the place. It was just a stone's throw away from the main road. There were big clean boulders around and it looked kind of an ideal place to sit around and have a moment of quietness.

Dustin parked the motorcycle and got down, helping her get down too. He led her to a boulder and sat down watching the clear water under the dazzling moonlight. Their legs brushed as they sat beside each other inhaling the fresh air and the feeling of each other's company.

"Why do you love me, Jade?" He asked her, staring at her creamy complexion which shone under the moonlight, her hair that cascaded down her back like spun gold. He couldn't remove his eyes from her face. Not that he wanted to.

"I don't know. I just do," she answered, almost in a whisper, her eyes looking away from his.

"Thank you for everything that you did for me and granny," he said, picking up her hand and kissing her knuckles. She shivered at the gentle kiss.

She looked into his eyes and saw his dark, intense stare that melted her inner resolve of not allowing him to kiss her. In fact, she wanted him to kiss her. They stared at each other like two tortured souls trying to get their moment of happiness with each other.

"I missed you Jade. I missed you very much," he whispered as he lowered his head. "Please don't deny me. I can't control myself anymore."

Jade's hands went around his neck to caress his hair at the nape of his neck. "Tell me what you want, Jade," he asked, his voice thick and husky.

"Kiss me, Dustin," she pleaded. It didn't take him a second and his mouth claimed hers in a searing hot kiss. This wasn't just a hungry kiss. It was branding. Like he was marking her as his. They kissed each other, forgetting the world around them, forgetting everything but each other.

When Dustin's mouth left hers to press a kiss on her neck, she closed her eyes and trembled like a leaf. His arm went around her, pulling her close.

"You have grown really ravishing," he commented, with a wink. His roving eye taking in her entire body.

"Shut up, you perv," she said, blushing and smacking his arm.

"What? It's the truth. Don't you like mine? I worked out only for you," he said, pulling up his sleeves and flexing his biceps to show her.

"Big deal. Every Tom, Dick and Harry has it," she said in a bored tone.

"Oh really? How many guys have you dated behind my back?"he asked, green with jealousy as he clenched his teeth.

"Wouldn't you like to know?" She teased and he stared at her.

"You've become bolder. I like it. I really like it," he confessed, with a grin.

"Granny told me you witnessed the murder. What were you doing here so late at night Jade? It could have been dangerous, you know, " he told her and she looked at her hands, unable to decide whether to tell him about her notebook.

"I lost something that night at your house, so I came back to get it," she confessed. She couldn't tell him about the notebook.

"Is this what you lost that night?" He asked, staring at her for her reaction as he pulled out her old, worn out notebook from his chest pocket. Jade gasped seeing her notebook after eight long years. All this time he had it with him?

She stared at him speechless. When she came back to her senses, she said shyly, "Yeah."

"It was my only companion for the last eight years. It made me feel that I was close to you. I slept with it and woke up with it, " he muttered as if in.a daze, staring at the notebook. When he looked up at her, she was lost in their chocolate brown depths. They held so much pain and something else which stirred her soul. She touched his cheek and he leaned into her touch.

"It's all over now, Dustin. I'm with you, am I not?"she comforted him. He closed his eyes and nodded.

"Don't leave me, ever, Jade, " he pleaded.

"I won't. But if I don't go home now, dad will start hunting for me with a gun," she said and he laughed.

"You're right. Let's get you home now," he said and they got up and climbed into the motorcycle.

They reached her house and he turned off his ignition. "Give me your car keys. I'll fix your tyre and have your car delivered here," he said. Jade handed him her car keys.

"Thanks, that would be a great help," she admitted.

"When is your work starting tomorrow?" He asked her.

"At 11 o'clock. Why?" She asked curiously.

"I'll come at 9 o'clock to pick you up. Spend some time at the restaurant. Granny misses you," he coaxed.

"Ok," she agreed and he grinned.

"Do I get a good night kiss?" He asked, hopefully.

"No, dad's watching us, " she told him and his eyes widened.

"Oh, where is he?" He whispered.

"You go now, please, " she pleaded.

"Ok. Be ready," he said and sped away. Jade grinned at his adorable ways. She would have kissed him good night but with her father watching them from his bedroom window, it wasn't a good idea. She would now get ready to answer her dad. Hope he isn't too mad at her.

Chapter Thirteen

Christopher Meyers stood at the foyer with his arms folded on his chest, his expression solemn just like the calm before an impending storm.

Jade unlocked the main door with her spare key and entered. She glanced at her dad and closed the door softly. Then turning around she faced him.

"Where are you coming from young lady?" He spoke in a stern voice.

"Work dad," she answered, calmly.

"Dustin Moore works with you?" He asked, frowning at her.

"My car had a flat tyre so he offered to drop me home, " she answered, looking him in the eye. She wasn't lying so there was no reason to be intimidated.

"I see. You are an hour and a half late," he stated, looking at the wall clock.

"Yeah, we talked dad," she said, calmly.

"Are you two dating?" He asked, looking at her suspiciously.

"No dad. We just talked," she confessed.

"Whatever you do, don't get pregnant. I have a good reputation here," he stated firmly.

Jade rolled her eyes. She knew that and she was mature enough not to allow that to happen. "I know dad," she assured him.

"Let's eat dinner and go to bed. It's late already," said her dad leading the way to the dining room where Stella was serving dinner.

"That would be all Stella. You can go home now," said her dad and Stella nodded happily. After she left, they ate dinner and went up their rooms to sleep.

The next morning Jade took a shower and went downstairs to make coffee. "Make one for me too," said her dad, picking up the newspaper from the front porch. He closed the main door and sat down at the table to read it. Jade brought coffee and cookies to the table and sipped hers. Her dad too sipped his coffee.

It was just seven-thirty in the morning. Jade was checking her emails when the doorbell rang. Who could it be so early in the morning? Stella came at 9 o'clock in the morning.

Jade went to open the door. She stood rooted to the spot, seeing Dustin standing there, grinning at her. "You?" She asked incredulously.

"Yeah, I couldn't sleep. So I showered and came here to fetch you," he said, scratching his head looking like a naughty school boy doing what he shouldn't be doing.

"Who are you talking to Jade?" Asked her dad. Dustin's eyes grew wide and he went to hide behind the pillar on the porch.

"Dustin, it's just dad. Come inside," she coaxed, holding his hand and pulling him inside the house.

"Dad, Dustin's here to take me to see granny. I didn't visit for a week," she informed her dad.

"Come join us for coffee, Dustin," he invited and Dustin nodded,"Thank you, sir," he said and sat opposite her dad. Jade went to get him coffee.

When she was gone, Mr Meyers asked him,"Have you received the compensation from the government?"

"No, sir, it will take a month," he informed.

Mr Meyers nodded in understanding,"Yeah, these things take time. So, what do you plan to do with the money?" He asked, curiously.

"I'll be building two more floors above the restaurant sir and turn it into a small motel. We have sanction for the floors but didn't have money to build," he said and her dad nodded appreciatively.

"But you would require more money for that," he stated.

"Yeah, I thought about that. My maternal uncle James Caldwell left some money to me last year when he died. I have spoken to Jayson. He will help me acquire it," he informed her father.

"That's wonderful news," he appreciated.

"Yeah, it's a big amount. I can buy a house and save the rest in the bank," he told him.

"That's very good news but keep it to yourself. Money brings out the worst in people. You never know what people can do for money," he advised.

"Yes, sir," Dustin said as Jade brought him his coffee and some cake. They talked about the two cases some more and then Dustin took his leave.

"Do drop in sometimes when you're free Dustin. Would love to talk more," said her father.

"Yes sir, I will," Dustin promised.

"Call me uncle Chris. Quentin and I had studied together since our freshman year. We were good friends," informed her dad. Quentin Moore was Dustin's dad. He was a general physician at the Travis Springs state general hospital where he met Dustin's mom, Dana. She was a nurse there. During Dustin's final year at school they met with a fatal accident while returning from Alabama where Dustin's uncle James Caldwell lived. He was the only brother and the only living family of his mom.

"I know uncle Chris, granny told me many times. You used to come home when dad was younger and at school," said Dustin and Christopher Meyers smiled in remembrance.

"Yeah, those were the days," he stated. "Anyways, you both carry on now. I'll go take a shower," he said, getting up to go to his room.

Jade cleared the table and ran upstairs to get her handbag and then after kissing her dad's cheek, left with Dustin.

They climbed onto Dustin's Ford F-150 and sped off towards the restaurant. "Weren't you supposed to come at 9 o'clock?" She asked, looking at him.

He grinned without looking towards her. "What can I do? You kept popping up in my dreams and I just couldn't sleep. So I took a cold shower at 5 in the morning and have been fidgeting around since then," he informed her and she sat with her mouth open wide.

"Oh, you could have counted sheep and slept," she suggested.

"I didn't want to. We were doing so many interesting things, who wanted to count sheep in the middle of it all?" He stated, glancing at her briefly to wink.

"What things?" She asked, frowning.

"Oh, well. I was on top of you and was eating you..," he started and she screamed covering her ears with her hands.

"Shut up, you perv. I don't want to hear," she said with a red tomato face.

"What? We will do it soon," he stated matter of factly.

"No we won't," she said firmly.

"Yes, we will. How else will we have our children, silly," he stated and she stared at him dumbfounded.

"Our children? We're not even married. Dad will kill me if we produce children before marriage, " she said, glaring at him.

"Oh we will marry too, give me a little time, baby," he said, with a wide wide smile.

"Baby? I like it," she said smiling back.

They reached the restaurant and Jade jumped down and went into the kitchen. Dustin parked his truck and followed, whistling a merry tune as there were no customers.

"He looks so happy with you around. I'm so thankful to you dear. Do drop in once a day, else he goes crazy. He's whipped with you dear," said granny and Jade nodded.

"I will granny. But don't tell him," she said with a naughty smile. Granny chuckled. Jade helped with the breakfast items on the menu. Dustin dropped by every now and then when the restaurant was a little empty. Finally he placed Richardson at the counter and walked into the kitchen.

"Granny, I'm hungry," he said, opening every pot and pan for food. Granny slapped his hand away.

"Those are for customers. You go to our kitchen. There's pasta. Heat it and eat. Take Jade with you. She could also do with some food. She's so skinny. She needs more food," said granny, shaking her head.

Dustin grinned mischievously. "Sure granny. You're right. She needs to eat. Come on Jade, let's go and eat," he said, catching her wrist and pulling her away with him before granny changed her mind.

He didn't leave her till he opened the door of his apartment and led her inside, closing the door after him. "Who wants food when I can have you?" He said with a mischievous glint in his eyes.

Jade's eyes went wide. What was he planning to do?

Chapter Fourteen

He placed his arms on either side of her, trapping her. His eyes were dark pools of desire as he stared intensely at her mouth. "Kiss me Jade," he whispered. "I've waited all night for this, please," he pleaded.

She touched his lip with her thumb, slowly stroking it as he groaned in agony. His sharp intake of breath was indication enough that he was aroused beyond thinking. He took her thumb into his mouth and sucked it. She pulled it out of his mouth as if burnt.

His one hand caught the nape of her neck, angling it as his mouth captured hers in a passionate kiss. His tongue softly glided into her open mouth, licking every recess, tasting her, biting her. It wasn't enough. His other hand slipped down to her hips and pulled her close to his body. It was a hard and deep kiss that made her long for more.

His slightly rough hand caressed the creamy skin of her neck and shoulders. He was relentless. He wanted to taste more of her. His mouth trailed down to her neck and pressed a hot possessive kiss there.

She shivered as his stubble grazed her soft neck. "Mine, only mine," he said against her skin. Her heart hammered against her chest. Her head was spinning at the intensity of his kisses. She closed her eyes to gather herself together as he continued his attack on her neck.

"Say that you're mine, Jade," he prompted.

"I'm yours Dustin, you know it," she whispered breathlessly.

His stomach grumbled and she laughed. "The lion's hungry, let's eat," she said, tweaking his nose. He reluctantly left her, happily grinning at the mark he left on her neck.

"Ok, let's eat," he breathed, going to the kitchen and taking out the pasta. Jade followed and helped him warm it. They served themselves and sat at the table to eat it.

"We'll continue after eating," he said, looking smugly at her.

"No we won't. Granny will come to check us if we don't go back," she reminded him.

"Oh no, she won't," he said, grinning with a twinkle in his eye.

"I've a job to go to," she told him.

"We'll see, " he said with a wink.

Dustin cleaned the table while Jade washed the dishes. She was about to turn when Dustin came from behind her and trapped her between himself and the kitchen sink. His arm went around her waist and pulled her against his body, with her back against his front.

"Jade, can I see you afterwards? After work? I've become obsessed with you," he said, inhaling her neck, his lips roughly skimming her shoulder.

"Yes," she said, breathlessly. She could feel the butterflies in her stomach at his nearness. Her heart sang at his words.

Yet he didn't leave her. He embedded his face in her neck and stayed there. "What do you do to me Jade? I just can't stay without you. I want you to stay in my arms, every minute, every second, all the time," he whispered, showering soft kisses all over her neck, jawline and shoulders.

Jade trembled with longing. She didn't want to leave his side either. She slowly turned to face him. He pulled her close and lowered his head to plant a kiss at the corner of her mouth, working its way to capture her full lips. He kissed her longingly, hard and deep.

Then letting her go, he took a deep breath and asked, "Will you go on a date with me tomorrow, Jade?"

"Yes, when?" She asked curiously.

"Tomorrow I'll pick you up at 7 o'clock in the morning?" He asked hopefully.

Jade grinned excitedly. "Ok." Tomorrow being a Saturday, she didn't have work to go to. Dustin smiled excitedly at the prospect of going out on his first date with her.

They locked the main door and went back to the restaurant. Granny looked up at the two excited faces. "Did you like it?" She asked Jade.

Jade's eyes widened and cheeks turned tomato red,"Umm, like what, granny?" She asked, blushing more. How did she know how Dustin kissed her and how much she liked his kisses? Granny chuckled and Dustin just stared Jade,.mesmerised by her. He could watch her whole day and night without tiring.

"I'm talking about the pasta, dear," granny said with a laugh.

"Oh, that," breathed Jade. "I loved it, thank you granny, " she said, hugging granny. Granny hugged her back, chuckling at Dustin's jealous reaction to their hugging.

"I'll get going now granny, duty calls," she said, with a smile and picking up her handbag left the kitchen with Dustin following her.

"See you in the evening," he said and she nodded at him and rushed to the boutique. She could sense Dustin checking out her backside from where he was standing and watching her.

The whole day she spent dreaming about his kiss, his dark chocolate brown eyes and the way he stared at her. At the end of the day, she could get very little work done. Her mind kept revolving around Dustin, her Dustin. Finally she completed her work and left the boutique, waving at Valentina who was also about to lock it up and leave. Brittany, who owned the boutique was related to Valentina and she was away on a vacation with her husband and kids.

Walking towards her car, she saw Dustin, leaning against it with the keys in his hand. How could someone look so gorgeous as well as adorable at the same time? His face broke into a mischievous grin, the moment he saw her. She grinned back at him. "You fixed my car?" She asked excitedly.

"Yeah, but I want a kiss in return," he negotiated, holding her car keys high up. He couldn't believe how pathetic he sounded but how could he help himself when all he wanted was to kiss her senseless.

"Please Dustin, everyone's looking. This is a marketplace and everyone knows dad," she said, embarrassed.

"Then I will take my kiss from you tomorrow. Be ready at 7 in the morning. Wear comfortable clothes and carry a swimsuit," he said, his mischievous look back on his face as she looked at him curiously.

"Why? Where are we going?" She couldn't help but feel curious.

"You'll see tomorrow. If you kiss me, I could tell you," he winked and waited with a mischievous glint in his eyes.

"See you tomorrow then," she said and his face fell as she climbed into the car and drove off. She could have given him his kiss but with everyone knowing her dad, she couldn't take the risk. Her dad would get furious if he found out. But where was he taking her so early in the morning? She was very curious but there was only one way to find out now. Wait for tomorrow.

Going home, she sat down to dinner with her dad. "Dad, tomorrow I have a date with Dustin at 7 o'clock in the morning, " she informed him.

"Where are you going so early in the morning?" He asked, frowning.

"A nature trail or adventure camp maybe. I have to dress casually. That's all he divulged, " she said and her dad nodded.

"Just be careful and be home on time," said her dad in a strict parental tone.

"Sure dad," she promised, thankful that she got her permission without much explanation.

She went to bed after packing a small backpack excited to spend the day with Dustin.

Chapter Fifteen

S he showered and got ready by 6:15 in the morning. Her dad insisted that she eat something before going. So she had a sandwich and coffee and was ready to go. Dustin came at 6:50 and rang the bell.

Jade rushed to open. "Hi, I'm ready," she said excitedly, taking him in. He looked so good in a pair of blue denims that hugged his thick legs. A black tee shirt with a leather jacket made him look like a bad boy out on a forbidden adventure. His dark brown eyes shone with excitement and his eyes took in her wholly, from head to foot and back up.

"Hey, you're looking too gorgeous for your own good," he remarked only for her ears though, with a wink. He sauntered through into her living room to greet her dad.

"Good morning uncle Chris. Can I take Jade out for the day?" He asked politely with his hands fidgeting behind his back.

"You already are, young man. Just take care of her. I'm sure you will," her dad said with a smile.

"Yes, uncle Chris. I will. Rest assured and we will return on time," he promised.

"God bless you. Off you go, then. Enjoy," said her dad, picking up his newspaper.

"Thank you uncle," said Dustin happily.

Jade kissed her dad's cheek. "Bye dad, thank you," she said and her dad patted her head indulgently.

They went out and climbed onto Dustin's Ford F-150. He switched on the ignition and manoeuvred it out of her driveway onto the road.

"Now tell me where we're going," she asked, turning sideways towards him.

He smirked. "Not so easily. You escaped the deal yesterday. Kiss me if you want to know," he negotiated again.

She rolled her eyes. He was still stuck on that note? "How can I?" She asked and he simply shrugged.

"Ok, you win. When we cross Travis Springs?" She asked him, shyly.

His grin widened as if he won a prize. "Sure," he agreed. "Are you carrying a swimsuit?" He asked, with another glint in his eyes.

"Yeah, I'm wearing my bikini," she said, suspiciously. Why was he harping on it? So, they were going near a waterbody.

"That's even better. I can't wait to see you in it," he said excitedly. Jade rolled her eyes. Men! So they weren't going near the water or what? Did he just want her to parade in her bikini?

They crossed the marketplace and headed towards the highway. "How far is this place?" She asked.

"Ohno, you don't get any hint. First my kiss," he said, shaking his head and driving around the bend and heading south-west. She stomped her foot in frustration. Dustin simply grinned wickedly knowing very well how frustrated she was feeling.

Jade took in the scenery as they crossed Travis Springs and headed towards the suburbs. "We've crossed Travis Springs," he informed her.

"Oh," she said, her cheeks turning red.

Dustin looked around for a place to park the truck. He'd been going crazy since last night. He needed a kiss. It was his only medicine.

At last he found an ideal place. He diverted the truck off the highway onto a narrow deserted trail. After driving a little, he parked the truck beside a pecan tree. Switching off the ignition, he turned towards her,"Kiss me, now," he demanded, looking at her with the same dark, desire filled eyes and erratic breathing.

She leaned forward and was about to kiss his cheek, when he turned his head towards her,"A kiss on the cheek doesn't count. Only on the lips count," he said in a raspy, desire filled voice.

Jade rolled her eyes. He lost his patience and simply unbuckled her seat belt and pulled her onto his lap, straddling her facing him. He inhaled her deeply. "You smell so good," he said, his face near her neck.

He leaned and grazed her neck in a feather light kiss, inhaling more. Jade trembled, her nipples standing erect through the soft bikini top that she was wearing underneath her tee shirt. Her hands went up to caress his soft hair. It went up in a mohawk when she brushed it with her fingers. A soft chuckle escaped her.

"What are you doing with my hair, baby?" He asked, looking at himself in the mirror with horror. "Ugh," he pouted.

She fixed his hair and it flopped over his forehead making him look like a cute little boy. Again a chuckle escaped her and he frowned. She got down from his lap, and burst out laughing, seeing his hair. He looked at the mirror and brought out a comb from his pocket. After combing himself to his satisfaction, he glared at her.

"You will be punished for this, just you wait," he threatened in mock disapproval and Jade grinned.

He started the ignition and drove onto the main highway again. "So my kiss stays pending. And the deal is renewed. Three kisses are due now," he said, with a smirk, happy with the deal.

"How three?" She asked with wide eyes.

"First, for fixing your car, second is for telling you where we're going and the third for messing my hair," he informed with a mischievous grin.

"Oh, I don't need you to tell me where we're going, so that means you get only two," she said, with a grin.

"Fine, give me two. Then there's the punishment you will get," he said, with a smirk.

Jade rolled her eyes and looked out of the window. "Remind me why I even love you," she mumbled.

"You just do since I'm irresistible, " he said, smiling widely.

"I'm more," she stated, giving him a dirty glance.

"That you are. You don't know what I do to you in my dreams," he said, smirking.

"I don't want to hear," she covered her ears and he laughed.

"Don't listen. You can watch when we do it," he said, leaning a little towards her.

"Shut up or or I won't kiss you," she threatened.

"I will make you kiss me, darling," he said as they turned onto a side trail, narrower than the highway but in good condition.

"This is it? We've reached? Yay," said Jade excitedly looking around. It was a deserted trail amidst lots of trees and shrubs. After driving through a little distance they could hear, the sound of herons, egrets and woodpeckers and kingfishers. The splashing sound of water could be distinctly heard too.

In another three minutes, they could see a huge water body filled up to the brim with water shimmering from the sun's rays reflected upon it. All sorts of birds flew around the tall pecan trees surrounding the area. Lush green grassy banks made it a picture perfect place.

Jade gasped at the beauty of it all. "It's heavenly, Dustin. Where are we?" She asked, her eyes wide with wonder.

"This is the Travis Bayou, fed by the Travis river. It's a popular paddling trail here. Migratory birds come here during Spring and Winter," he informed her.

"So are we camping here?" She asked looking around.

"No, have patience," he said driving on along the bayou till they reached a loop. They moved along it towards the furthest side and deviated towards a smaller stream. It led to a small lake. The grassy slopes housed a small log cabin. The place was almost covered with tall pecan trees creating a secluded heaven.

"This is the most beautiful place on earth," she gasped, as he stopped the truck beside the cabin and helped her out.

She walked towards the lake and inhaled the fresh air filled with the smell of ripe pecans. "What's this place called?" She asked, closing her eyes at the tranquillity of the air.

"Welcome to Pecan Creek," he said, "It's ours."

Chapter Sixteen

J ade stared at him in astonishment, "Ours?" She asked in confusion.

"Yeah, I bought it last week," he informed her with a grin, procuring a key from his pocket and opening the cabin.

"How? I mean it must have cost a fortune," she asked, shocked by his statement.

"No actually, I got it at a discounted rate, " he informed, as they went inside the small cabin. There was a small partitioned area with a queen sized bed and a chest of drawers on one side of it and a dresser on the other side.

There was a small living area with a comfortable four seater sofa and an open kitchen with all electric appliances on the other side. A small two seater dining table occupied the side near the kitchen. There was a bathroom with a bathtub near the bedroom side.

"It's so cosy. I love it," she gushed, as she checked out the cabin. She could live here with her Dustin forever.

"I know. I could live here with you forever. So when my friend Seth wanted to sell it along with his house and move to Australia. I couldn't resist the deal," he said with a proud smile.

"Where did you get so much money from?" She asked, with eyes round like saucers.

Dustin grinned,"My mom's brother, James Caldwell left me a fortune when he died last year. Jayson helped me get half of it. The other half will take some time. I will also recieve some money from the government," he said.

"That's great news Dustin. So where did you buy a house? In Travis Springs or somewhere else?" She asked hesitantly.

"Right beside your dad's," he said and her mouth fell to the floor.

"What? There's Rosalie's parents house only next door. Wait! Are you talking about the house with a huge courtyard and spectacular swimming pool on the other side?" She asked with wide eyes. That was a luxurious and beautiful house she always stared at.

"Yes, you like it?" He asked, proudly.

"Like it? I love it. It's my dream house," she gushed and jumped up and kissed his cheek.

Dustin caught her and grinned happily. "It's our house now. Our children will grow up in it. You'll cook and wash for me," he said with dreamy eyes.

"Yeah. You'll do the dishes for me," she said with dreamy eyes.

He looked at her and smiled wickedly,"Only if you let me make love to you whole night, every night, " he stated.

Dumbfounded, she left him and walked towards the truck. "Let's carry out stuff inside, " she ordered and he saluted her and they carried their things inside.

"So much food? Are we staying here for a week?" She asked as they carried the food items inside.

"Wish we could. Let's eat whatever we can, rest we'll carry back home, " he said and she nodded.

When everything was brought in, she opened a can of lemonade and they drank it. There was a fruitcake which they shared.

"Let's go for a swim," he suggested. He opened his jacket and left it on the sofa. Then he simply took off his tee shirt in one jerk, staring at her all the while.

"What are you doing?" She whispered, staring wide eyed at him. His muscular body was turning her on so badly. She never felt like this with anyone else but one look at Dustin and she was a mass of nerves and longing. A deep longing to touch and be touched by him.

"Stripping for you my love. Are you enjoying the show?" He asked, coming closer as he unbuttoned his denims and let it fall to the floor, reavealing his navy blue swimming trunks.

She closed her eyes. His thick muscular legs and perfect six-pack body was too much for her. It made her long to be held in his arms. "It's your turn now," he said, his forefinger caressing her cheek softly.

"Close your eyes," she said and he shook his head.

"No, I can't. I need to see you, " he said in a hoarse whisper.

She unbuttoned her top slowly. "Here, let me," he said, removing her shaky fingers and unbuttoning her top, his slightly rough fingers brushing her soft skin. The top opened and he pulled it away, gasping as it revealed a nude lacy bikini top that strained her breasts, outlining them well.

His hot gaze made her nipples stand erect and his eyes darkened and he started breathing hard. This was Jade's favourite and only bikini. Since she last wore it four years back, it was a little tight for her.

She unbuttoned her denims and came out of it. Dustin stared at her tiny nude coloured bikini bottom with lace strings and felt himself go hard already. He came forward and picked her up in his arms. He actually wanted to touch her creamy skin.

"Dustin, I can walk. Put me down," she said, struggling.

He went out of the cabin and to the edge of the water. He waded down into the water with her on his shoulders as his hungry eyes took in her creamy butt cheeks. She really was too gorgeous for her own good. How would he control himself with her now?

"Stop staring," she hissed, uncomfortably squirming on his shoulder. Why did he have to carry her and then ogle at her butt?

"I can't. It's delicious," he said with a grin.

"Ugh, you're too much. Put me down, right now," she ordered irritatedly.

"As you wish," he released her slowly, her body moulding with his as he let her down.

She tried to wade away when he clutched at her. "Don't go far. I'm not sure how safe this place is. Stay close to me," he said trying to get hold of her waist to pull her close.

"Dustin, what have you done?" She yelled in panic. When he tried to catch her in panic, his fingers caught onto the bra strap and the flimsy strap came off altogether. She gasped in horror at her favourite bikini top floating away. She tried catching it, but the torn bra floated away further and she couldn't do a thing with Dustin holding her. She folded her hands on her bare breasts, blushing furiously with embarrassment. Why did such things happen only to her?

"Why did you wear such a teenie weenie thing?" He said, his eyes dancing with amusement as he kept glancing at her chest.

"Shut up and don't look. Get me a towel please," she said, not knowing what to do.

"I can't leave you alone here. What if a bear came and fell in love with you and took you away?" He said and her eyes went wide with horror. There were bears here?

She waded towards him, looking around her for a big bad bear. "There are bears here?" She squeaked.

"Yeah," he said in a hoarse and raspy voice. She glanced towards him. He was lost in her. His tortured look as he kept staring at her breasts was indication enough that he was very aroused. She had kept her chest covered with her arms.

He suddenly picked her up bridal style and her hand went to his shoulder for support. He stared at her exposed breasts and his sharp intake of breath made her conscious and she covered herself with her other hand.

He waded back with her in his arms. They reached the cabin and he went inside, locking the door.

"Please put me down, Dustin," she pleaded.

"No," he said roughly. He carried her to the bathroom and placed her on the counter. Then going to the cabinet, took out a soft clean towel. He came back and wrapped her with it, covering her.

"Kiss me now, Jade, " he ordered, coming closer to stand between her legs.

Chapter Seventeen

Jade held his face tenderly with both hands and gave a small peck on his lips. He pulled her close to his chest and angled her head and claimed her lips in a possessive kiss. It was a wild kiss, as if he dreamed about it the whole day. Maybe he had. Since the night before he had been asking for it. She kissed him back and he groaned with pleasure.

He pressed his body against hers as he kissed her more passionately. When he finally broke the kiss, he closed his eyes to steady his breath. Then resting his forehead against hers, he uttered the words that she had been craving to hear for the last eight years, "My jade, my love, my life." She was overwhelmed with emotions at his simple six words.

Before she could calm her nerves, he suddenly left her and stood with his back towards her. She looked at his back with concern. What did she do now? Did she do something to hurt him? "Dustin, have I done something to hurt you?" She asked, touching his shoulder.

His sharp intake of breath as he removed her hand confused her further. He slowly turned around. His breathing erratic, his pupils dilated and dark just like storm clouds. She could see his massive arousal hardly contained by his swimming trunks. She blushed furiously and lowered her lashes, not knowing what to do. "Are you ok?" She whispered.

"No, I'm not ok. I want to make love to you. I want to taste you. I want to be inside you. I'm tired of my dreams. They're driving me crazy, Jade. Are you ready for me?" He asked with a tortured look full of longing.

She was dumbfounded by his statement. She couldn't utter a single word. No one ever loved her or wanted her this way before. Was she ready for him? Maybe not yet. How would she tell him that? She didn't want to hurt him.

He took her quietness as a no. "Then give me a moment to calm myself please. I love you, I can wait for you. But once I get a taste of you, I won't stop. I will have you as and when I please," he said, turning away from her. "You can take a shower. I'll get your clothes." He added and disappeared out of the bathroom.

He returned with a body wash, her clothes and her backpack. "Here, " he said, handing them to her.

"Thank you, " she said and he nodded, leaving her and going to the kitchen.

Dustin felt happy that he could tell her that he loved her. He wanted to sing and dance with joy. He put on his denims and went out to catch a fish.

After fifteen minutes, he came back with a good catch. Jade was in the kitchen, chopping vegetables for a salad. He showed her the crappies that he caught and she squealed with delight.

He cleaned and cut into fillets for frying as Jade prepared the batter. Dustin had come prepared with the ingredients as Seth had informed him about the lake teeming with good catches.

Granny prepared them with avocado rice and cupcakes. Both of them prepared the meal together. "It seems we are already married," said Dustin, grinning.

Jade smiled. "I want to stay here with you. I don't want to go home," she pouted.

"Me neither but I promised your dad and I will keep it," he said. She pouted but respected his principles.

"Well, now that we've started dating, we can take our relationship a little further. Right?" He said, leaning towards her to bump her shoulder and wink.

"How?" she said with a smile.

"I'm doing everything the conventional way," he said, feeling proud. "Will you be my girlfriend?" He asked, formally.

"Yes, I already am," she agreed and Dustin grinned.

They clung to each other and stayed that way.

"Tomorrow renovation work will start at our new house," he informed her.

"That's wonderful news," she gushed.

"I want you to go down and check what renovations you want. Decide the colour schemes and any other changes you want," he told her and she nodded happily. She stood on her tiptoes and kissed his cheek and he smiled indulgently.

They finished cooking and enjoyed their meal at the table overlooking the serene lake waters. The natural, quiet setting made them appreciate the moment more. Dustin held her chin and fed her a bite. Jade too fed him a bite.

"We can go boating after lunch. What do you say?" He asked her with excitement.

"Yeah, I'd love to," she agreed. They finished eating and cleaned up everything.

They went outside to the paddle boat. Dustin untied it and climbed in helping her inside. They paddled all over the lake, exploring nooks and corners, watching birds, fishes and squirrels. Dustin captured beautiful pictures of her, of themselves and the nature around him. She didn't know he was so interested in photography.

After spending nearly two hours, they returned to their cabin. "I'm exhausted," she told him, flopping on the sofa. He too sat down beside her.

"I want you to work at the restaurant. Once the rest of the money comes in, we will be building two more floors and turn it into a motel. I want you and granny to check out the designs. You would need to market it also. So would you want to complete your internship at the restaurant?" He asked, hoping she would agree.

"My internship is complete. As it is they weren't paying me well. So yes, I will work at the restaurant with you and granny but not for a payment. I will help because I love you all and it is mine also," she said with so much conviction that Dustin gave in.

"Okay if that's how you want it. But then you have to accept anything granny and I give you," he stated and she agreed.

"So, when will you join? I can't wait. I need to see you everyday, " he asked impatiently.

"Give me this month. I will give my resignation tomorrow and then serve the notice period they specify," she requested.

"Alright, just this month. Next month onwards, you join us," he declared.

"Ok," she agreed.

They rested for an hour, just talking and then went out hand in hand for a walk, exploring the area. It felt so good, without a care in the world, simply enjoying each other's presence.

"Can we come here again, Dustin?" She asked.

"Why not? It's ours. Whenever you want, we can come," he said. They walked back to the cottage and sat down on the deck to watch the birds catch fish.

"Thank you for being in my life, Jade. There aren't many people who have been a constant in my life. I only had granny and now I have you," he said, staring at his hands, his voice choked with emotions.

Jade simply held his hand in hers,"You're parents loved you," she comforted.

"No, they only loved their work and their friends. They didn't have time for me. They wanted a huge mansion to show off and went beyond their means to buy the place. Every weekend they hosted parties and I was sent away to granny's house. My mom didn't want granny to live with us, so granny lived all alone in grandpa's house. It was in a bad condition but they didn't have time for her as well. When I turned 13, I left home to live with granny. My parents came to fight regularly but I didn't want to go back. Then one day they met with an accident and everything came to an end. They left a huge debt on my shoulders," he sighed, looking at her with pain in his eyes.

"I didn't know, Dustin. Thank the Lord that you have granny," she said, hugging him.

"When we move to our new house, I can't leave granny alone in that small apartment, Jade," he said, his voice cracking with the emotions he kept hidden in his soul.

"Of course we won't. I love granny too, Dustin. She'll be staying with us," she said, laying her head on his chest.

"You won't mind her staying with us?" He asked, incredulously.

"Never. She's our family. I love both of you," she said with conviction.

"Thank you Jade. I'm glad I found you," he said, as he pulled her onto his lap and kissed her gently yet lingeringly. It was kiss which made them know how much they loved each other. It was a soulful kiss. A kiss with lots of gentle exploration of each other's mouths.

It was late afternoon and they packed everything back into the truck. After locking the place properly they drove back home. On the way back, they had dinner at a roadside diner.

Dustin dropped Jade and with a kiss on her forehead, climbed onto his truck and drove back home, happily.

Chapter Eighteen

The next day, Jade emailed her resignation to Brittany McGregor, the owner of the boutique. She accepted it immediately, directing her to serve a 10 day notice period prior to discontinuation.

Jade didn't have a problem with that. It would save her 5 days before the month ended. In the evening, Dustin came to meet her. He wanted to take her to their new house. She agreed and they went to inspect.

They finalised where they wanted their bedroom as well as other details and discussed with the site engineer of the construction team. Jade selected the colour combination for the whole house.

Happy with their decision, they strolled around, hand in hand around the backyard, deciding upon the decorations.

"I'm getting a gazebo constructed. We'll have our marriage ceremony under it. What do you say?" Asked Dustin, as they walked hand in hand to the site where the gazebo was to be constructed.

"It's a wonderful idea. I love gazebos," she said, staring at the place where construction work would start from tomorrow.

"There'll be a kid's pool for our babies. We'll have lots of children," he said and she rolled her eyes.

"No, only 2. I can't produce so many," she said and his face fell.

"We'll see what destiny has decided for us," he said and she agreed. Her dad came over to check what was going on.

"I'm so glad you both would live next door, Dustin. I wouldn't be lonely ever," he said, with a smile.

"Yes dad, even Dustin's granny would be shifting in with us," she informed and her dad's smile widened.

"Really? That means lots of goodies to eat," he said with excitement. They all laughed.

Her dad gave some suggestions and they both agreed. Jade went home and Dustin went back to his restaurant.

"He's a very good boy. I'm proud of your choice, Jade, " her dad appreciated and Jade felt so proud of her Dustin. He thought about everyone in whatever he did.

The next ten days went by as she wrapped up her work at the boutique. She visited the restaurant every morning as before to help granny and chat with her about the new house, taking her opinions about the decor. Dustin took granny to the new house regularly to check the progress. Jade visited whenever she could. Once her tenure at the boutique was over, she became free to join Dustin's restaurant.

She had informed her dad of her decision and he accepted her decision. So on her first day, she happily got down from her car and entered the restaurant, her restaurant from now on.

Dustin grinned at her from the table in the kitchen where he was sitting and eating a pecan pie. Jade rolled her eyes and tried to grab a piece from him but he held it up. Then placed one in his mouth, opening it wide.

"Come and get it," he said, his eyes gleaming with mischief.

"Ewww, you're disgusting, " she said. He chewed and gobbled it up and grinned at her. How did he manage to maintain his figure after eating all that?

"Granny, don't you think he should share?" She glared at him. He grinned and dangled his legs, eating more.

Granny chuckled,"Dustin, give her a piece," she suggested.

"She can come to me and get it herself, " he suggested and Jade blushed like a tomato. He had no shame at all saying such things in front of his granny. How could she get the cake from his mouth in front of granny?

"No thanks," she said, pouting and going to the counter to chop the vegetables. Dustin got down from the table and walked up to her. He turned her around and fed her a piece. Then handing her the rest of the pie, he just tweaked her nose and winked.

"Enjoy the treat. I will take the payment later," he said and went away out of the kitchen to the counter with a smirk.

"He loves you too much, see?" Said granny and Jade grinned and fed her a piece too.

Jade was done with helping in the kitchen. Dustin led her to a small office room that he had built for her near a corner, just outside the restaurant towards the backside. There was a bay window and a desk in front of it with a computer and three chairs. A small potted plant on the window sill and a painting decorated the place. There was a cabinet for storage.

"This is your office for the time being. When you're not helping in the kitchen you can sit here and work. Submitting to search engines, posting reviews and marketing the restaurant. I had a website made. You can keep submitting the url for online marketing," he suggested and she nodded.

"I've got it. Don't worry, I'll start immediately, " she said, starting the computer.

He entered the password and informed her of it. "You can change the password if you want," he said.

"I'll leave you to it. But remember, my payment is due. I'll want it before you leave," he reminded her with a grin and left, closing the door behind him.

She smiled to herself. He really was so adorable. He had an office room built just for her. The next two hours, she was drowned in her work. Optimising their website with valid and important keywords for search engine recognition.

Granny came and sat down in front of her. "It's lunch time sweetheart," she said. "Come and eat with us," she invited and Jade felt her stomach grumble.

"When do you rest granny? You're in the kitchen since morning. I'm sure they can manage if you slept for two hours now. I can help if you tell me what to do," she suggested, concerned about her granny.

"Thank you dear. I'll tell you what needs to be done and rest after lunch. Does that make you happy?" She asked, getting up.

"Yes, very happy," said Jade, shutting her computer and going with granny to her apartment at the backside.

Dustin came in with a lot of extra food that hadn't been used at the restaurant and served the three of them. Even Jade helped him.

They ate up and forced granny to goto her room and rest. Granny instructed Jade what needed to be done. They cleaned up the dining table and the kitchen and went back to the restaurant. Jade went into the kitchen while Dustin handled the counter as the lunchtime rush kept them busy for the next three hours.

Jade suggested they keep a customer review book near the counter where each customer could give suggestions and comments. The suggestions could be implemented upon and the best reviews could be uploaded onto their website. They also decided to take a photograph of the signature dishes of their restaurant and post it on their website.

After a day's hard work, Jade kissed granny who had returned to the kitchen in the evening. Before she could reach the front door, Dustin followed her and pulled her along with him to the backside near the entrance to their apartment.

"Give me my payment before you go," he breathed onto her face. He pinned her to the door and blocked her with his body rubbing against hers.

"Dustin, someone will see us," she whispered.

"I don't care. I will die if you don't kiss me now," he said with such longing that Jade gave in. Her arms went around his neck as she pulled him close.

"I love you Dustin," she whispered, and gently brushed her lips to his. He groaned and claimed her lips possessively, branding her more with his hot touch. The fire inside him made him crazy for her but he had promised to wait till she was ready.

His tongue glided inside, tasting her sweetness as his hands bunched around her hips and pulled her close to his body, not leaving an inch between themselves.

"I want you Jade. Are you ready for me?" He asked her in a hoarse whisper.

"Yes, Dustin," she answered and he kissed her more passionately.

"Go out with me tomorrow night for dinner?" He asked her.

"Yes," she answered.

"It's a date," he promised.

"Hmm," she said.

He left her reluctantly and she went home looking forward to tomorrow's date.

Chapter Nineteen

The next whole day, Dustin kept reminding her of their date. Even granny came to know that they were going on a date. She told them stories of her date with Dustin's grandpa. They held their stomach and rolled with laughter when granny told them how she poured wine over grandpa's head for trying to kiss her.

Jade was forced to go home an hour early to get ready for her date. She chose a beautiful off shoulder black skater dress with short sleeves and high-low hemline. She curled her hair and let it fall around her in soft curls. Clipping a pair of sterling silver earrings with black diamond studs to match her outfit. She was ready when tye doorbell rang.

Stella announced Dustin's arrival and she went downstairs to greet him. His mouth dropped as he kept staring at her. Her dad was at Jayson's house for dinner.

"You're looking very beautiful, Jade. I could eat you for dinner," he commented and she smiled.

"So are you," she said, taking in his pale blue dress shirt and black slacks and black blazer. His hair might have been gelled as it was combed to perfection.

"I don't mind you eating me," he teased.

"I didn't mean that," she answered, with red cheeks.

He helped her to his Ford F-150 and going towards the driver's seat, climbed in. He maneuvered the truck towards the main road.

After a while they reached the marketplace. "Where are we going?" She asked as he parked the car in front of his restaurant. Jade was confused as he led her into his own restaurant.

"We'll have our date here? What about when you have customers? Who would do their billing?" She asked, curiously looking at the empty restaurant.

The whole restaurant was decorated with red heart shaped balloons and satin ribbons. A single table was draped with white floor length tablecloth. There was a silver vase with red roses as a centrepiece. Silver cutlery adorned the table. Jade gasped at the beauty of it all.

"Wow, it's beautiful. Who decorated this place? It wasn't there when I left?" She said, glancing towards Dustin, who was scratching his head undecided whether to tell her or not.

"Well, I had it decorated for our date," he confessed and Jade jumped with joy.

"If there are customers, Richardson will handle them. Let's enjoy our dinner," he said, leading her to the beautifully decorated table.

They sat and wine was served along with appetizers. There were beef sausage pot-stickers and mozzarella sticks in hot spinach artichoke dip.

"These are granny's recipes. Right? She could have joined us," said Jade.

"Granny's tired. She had an early dinner and went to bed," said Dustin.

"These are delicious, " gushed Jade, as she licked the dip off her lips. "You have some dip on your lips," she told Dustin who tried to lick it.

"Here let me," she offered, brushing his lips with her thumb. His sharp intake of breath indicated that he loved the touch of her fingers on his lips. He caught her hand and licked the dip off.

"Your staff would be watching us," she breathed.

"Let them. They know we are together, " he informed and Jade nodded.

The main course was brought in. Granny's special Texas chicken casserole doused with hot sauce over the top. They served stir fried asparagus and pan seared potato wedges on the side. It was the most mouth watering meal that she had in decades.

"It's delicious. The best that I had in ages," she said, honestly.

"I know, I didn't want you to have dinner anywhere else, but here, to savour granny's dishes," he said.

They enjoyed their meal amidst easy discussions regarding their house and it's progress. They were glad that the house would be ready in 15 more days.

Dustin informed her that he had received the rest of the inherited sum. The compensation money has been sanctioned and he would receive it by next month.

The dessert was served. Strawberry shortcake which was Dustin's favourite.

"I can't eat a crumb more. I'm so full," said Jade and Dustin grinned.

"Then it's time," he said and gestured towards the chef in the kitchen who was peeping at them through the glass aperture.

"Time for what?" She asked in confusion.

Suddenly music started and she turned around to see their chef strumming a guitar. She stared around with wonder. What was going on? Dustin went down on one knee in front of her. She gasped when realisation struck.

"I was crushing on you from the moment I saw you at the party that day. I didn't realise I was in love with you too. I realised when you were separated from me and I was sentenced for 15 long years. I was broken and shattered Jade. I didn't have any hope of ever seeing you in this wretched life. But your love saved me and here I am contemplating a future with you. It's so surreal, like a dream come true. So will you make this dream last forever? Will you marry me Jade?" He asked with his eyes shining with raw emotions.

"Yes, Dustin. Not only you, it's a dream come true for me too," she answered. He took out a box from his pocket and opened it. A small jade ring with diamonds around it sparkled from inside the box. He took it out and placed it onto her finger.

"I had it made especially for you, " he said, proudly.

"It's the most beautiful thing I've ever possessed Dustin. I love it," she gushed.

Suddenly loud claps filled the air as all their staff came out to congratulate them. Even granny came to congratulate them. They chatted some more and granny went back to her apartment.

Dustin and Jade left the restaurant. They went to their favourite spot beside the gurgling brook where he had taken her before to talk. They sat, hand in hand under the moonlit sky, staring ahead at the water rushing past.

"When are we getting married?"she asked him.

"In a fortnight? Our house should be ready by then," he said.

"Ok. But we need to announce to my family," said Jade. "Tomorrow there is our monthly get together at home and everyone would be present. Would you come over Dustin? We could announce our plans to my whole family," she suggested.

"Fine, I'll be there," confirmed Dustin. They kissed under the moonlight and then reluctantly got up to go home. Dustin dropped her and kissing her forehead drove off to his house, whistling a happy tune.

Chapter Twenty

The next day Jade was busy at home, helping Stella with the food. She had already informed her dad about their engagement. She told him that Dustin would attend the get together to announce their engagement to the whole family.

She had gone to the restaurant to work but came home early to help prepare dinner. By evening all the work was done. She showered and put on a beautiful sleeveless black crepe dress with an a-line silhouette and small pleats on the skirt. Leaving her hair untied, she went downstairs to give last minute finishing touches to everything.

Karen and Jayson came in with their twins. Jade greeted all of them and the kids jumped on her. "Give me a kiss first Ray and Val, only then you get my special cookies," she said to the twins who started demanding her cookies the moment they entered.

"There they start again," said Karen,"They've been at it the whole way here," she said, rolling her eyes.

The twins kissed Jade and received a small goodie bag full of her special cookies that she learnt from granny. When the kids were gone, Jaden and Rosalie came in with their twins, Andrea and Jace.

Their dad came out of his room and hugged everyone. The four year old twins rushed to their grandpa to show him their new action figures.

Dustin came in shyly and Jade went to greet him. She placed her hand possessively in the crook of his arm and led him inside. Everyone gave them knowing glances. Rosalie grinned and came towards them.

"I can see that you two are together now," she commented with a grin.

"Yes Rosalie, all credit goes to you,"Jade said, with a grateful smile. Then she turned to Dustin and introduced her,"Dustin, meet Rosalie, Jaden's wife. It's because of her that we are together. When I told her of your imprisonment, she convinced Jaden and Jayson to reopen your case to make me happy," said Jade, happily.

"Hi Rosalie, thanks for everything that you've done for me and for us," he thanked her sincerely.

"Oh, it's nothing. I'm glad that you both are together," said Rosalie.

Juliette and Xavion came in with their sons Xandros and Alexander and hugged Jade excitedly. "Are you getting hitched?" She whispered and Jade nodded. She introduced Dustin to them. After a little chat, Dustin went forward to greet her dad and two brothers and Xavion. Juliette, Jade and Rosalie went to Karen to catch up on the latest gossip.

Afterwards, they laid the table and summoned everyone to dinner. Her dad addressed everyone as was the ritual every time they gathered.

"Thank you for making it here tonight, children. I look forward to these moments with all of you throughout the month. It's the only time when the whole family gets to bond together. This month we have a special person with us, he's already a part of our family. He's also the son of a very dear childhood friend of mine. Everyone, meet Dustin Moore. He's also Jaden's classmate in school. Dustin has an announcement to make. So, thank you for being there for my Jade, Dustin. Go ahead and announce your engagement," said Christopher Meyers.

Dustin smiled at his uncle Chris,"Thank you uncle Chris. It's actually an honour to be sitting here with all of you. We have already bonded in the last 2 hours that we spend together, today. You already know now that Jade and I love each other profoundly. We have gone through many ups and downs and at last are together. We just got engaged last night. We are pleased to announce that we plan to get married in a fortnight," Dustin announced and everyone congratulated them.

They all started planning their wedding while enjoying the sumptuous meal that Stella and Jade had prepared.

Dustin's house would be ready in 10 days as they have started working overtime on it. They planned to have the wedding ceremony under the gazebo as planned.

The reception would take place in their dad's backyard like always. The guest list was drawn up and their dad called the same wedding planner who planned all their weddings perfectly.

So the dinner ended on an excited note and everyone promised to coordinate their outfits.

"Rosalie, will you be my matron of honour?" Asked Jade and Rosalie grinned.

"I thought you'd never ask," she said, teasing her.

So, Juliette and Karen would be her bridesmaids while the children would be the ring bearers and flower girls. They all planned to goto Brittany's boutique to get their wedding dresses stitched.

A week flew by and their wedding dresses were ready. The decorations were still going on. Granny and Jade regularly visited their new home. In 2 days, the work would be over and they could shift. Jade went to work in the restaurant everyday. She was happy with her decision to join her family's business.

Dustin received a lump sum compensation package from the government and he was happy. He would have the renovation and construction work started after the wedding.

They would retain the apartment at the backside in case granny wanted to rest while working in the kitchen. They could relax and take a lunch break there.

The wedding preparations were all done and the day of the wedding approached. Dustin's house was ready to move in and he was staying the night at his new house to arrange the stuff. Granny would shift by tomorrow. The wedding was in two days and she was excited as ever.

Her dad was in Austin to get some stuff for the wedding and stayed over at Juliette's house. He would arrive with them tomorrow morning.

Jade locked her house and went over to Dustin's house to check whether he needed help in arranging things. She pressed the doorbell and waited. When no one opened, she again pressed the doorbell and was about to return to her house, when the door opened. She was pulled inside hurriedly and the door locked.

She gasped at the sight of Dustin wearing only a towel around himself. "Sorry, you were taking a shower? I'll come back later," she said, turning to open the door and disappear.

"Oh no, you don't get to run away this time, baby," he said in a raspy tone. She looked at him curiously. What was wrong with him? One look at him filled her with a deep seated longing to be in his arms, to love and be loved.

He pulled her into his arms, harshly, and lowering his head, captured her lips in a wild kiss. His hungry mouth, bit, tasted, sucked her mouth, plundering it's sweet depths. Her hands caressed his hard torso and he hissed at her feather soft touches.

Breaking the kiss, he picked her up and walked away to their bedroom. She kissed his neck and he groaned. "Do you realise what you're starting Jade?" He breathed.

"Yes," said Jade, longingly.

"Are you ready for me? I can't control this time," he confessed.

Epilogue

H e carried her to their bed and deposited her gently. He opened his towel and she closed her eyes.

He climbed on top of her and pulled her hands away, gently. "I want you to see me, to touch me," he whispered, his hand picking hers up and placing them on his body for her to caress.

He gently opened her shorts and panties. Then he pulled her top over her head and discarded it. He unclasped her bra in one smooth move and discarded that too.

He stared at her naked body minutely, his fingers caressing her whole body sending delicious shivers all over her. "You're so beautiful and you're all mine," he murmured as if in a trance. His head dipped as he claimed one nipple and started sucking like a baby while his other hand stroked all over her. Jade closed her eyes at the pleasurable tingles that she felt all over. She was a throbbing mess already and he hadn't even started his love making.

His mouth traced down to her abdomen and down, tasting her wet innermost portion, his tongue delving into the deepest folds as he thrust it continuously in and out of her. Jade fisted on his hair, pushing him more into her as she moaned with continuous pleasure. Dustin continued with his fingers, plunging inside and out of her throbbing wetness till she released her juices into his fingers.

They made wild love the whole night and slept in each other's arms. It was the best night of their lives.

The next day, Jade had to return to her house early as granny was about to arrive with Richardson. They had shifted mostly everything they needed to this house, keeping some of their stuff in the apartment for emergency use.

Her dad and Juliette's family arrived around lunchtime. The next few days were very hectic with all her siblings and the children coming into their house. She went over to Dustin's house and helped them arrange the stuff around. They didn't want pre-wedding parties so everyone agreed and simply bonded with each other over lunch and dinner. Rosalie's parents too came over and helped with everything.

Granny thanked Christopher Meyers for standing by her and providing her with financial support during the time that Dustin was away. Jade's mouth fell. Her dad helped his family during their time of need? She just got up from her chair and gave him a big hug,"You're the best dad, ever," she said kissing his cheek.

Finally the day of the wedding arrived and the wedding planner got several attendants to get the bridal party ready. Some helped the children, others helped the bridesmaids and the matron of honour.

Two attendants helped her get ready. She wore a lace applique wedding gown with full illusion sleeves, and a sweetheart neckline. The fitting bodice was full of floral appliques all over. The full skirt with a chapel train gave the gown a romantic look complete with floral appliques all over the skirt.

They fixed her hair away from her face with an applique accessory and left the rest untied just as Dustin liked it. Her veil was kept simple with a single matching applique border. Her dad gave her a pair of beautiful diamond encrusted platinum earrings.

Dustin's granny gave her a crystal pendant with two hearts joined together as a symbol of their union. It was a gift from grandpa and she had treasured it to give to the woman her Dustin loved. Jade was touched by the love that was showered upon her.

Her bridesmaids wore mauve one shoulder floor length chiffon dresses with pleating at the bodice and the waistline. Rosalie's dress was two shades deeper than the bridesmaids. Jayson, Xavion and Jaden wore classic charcoal tuxedos with white dress shirts and black bows and black Dunbar shoes.

It was time for the wedding ceremony to start and her father came into her room. It was a very emotional moment. Her dad had tears of happiness in his eyes. "I wish your mom would have been alive to see this day, sweetie. This is the last wedding of the family, the next wedding will be when Jayson's children grow up. Time flies so fast. I wish you all the happiness in the world. This time I won't miss you much as you're just going next door," he said with a smile.

Jade hugged him,"Thank you for everything dad. I'm really lucky to have you," she said, smiling.

"It's time to get you married, let's go," said her dad leading her down the stairs and out of the house to Dustin's garden where they would be wed under the gazebo.

The gazebo was beautifully decorated with red heart shaped balloons and vines. White roses were bunched together and decorated to frame the altar. Ceremony benches were arranged in front of the gazebo for the guests.

White petals were strewn all along the aisle. Jade didn't want everyone to go overboard with the decorations. She wanted everything subtle and simple.

She stood waiting for the bridal procession to begin. Dustin stood at the altar with Jaden, his best man and the marriage officiant. Their eyes met and Jade took a deep breath seeing how handsome he looked in a classic black tuxedo with a white dress shirt and black bow. He smiled at her and her nervousness disappeared immediately.

The procession started and soon she was standing at the altar with her Dustin to start the wedding ceremony. It was a moment that they had waited for long. They became one in the eyes of God, ready to start a new life together. Dustin kissed his wife and after the wedding ceremony was over, they all left to enjoy the reception party.

The next three hours went by like a whirlwind. Dancing their first dance amidst lots of cheering, the speeches, the cake cutting and the dinner.

At last they were free to escape to their own world. Dustin drove her to their little log cabin in Pecan Creek for a week-long honeymoon. He had appointed Stella's sister Mary as their housekeeper back at home to take care of granny.

They ultimately found their eternal love after many ups and downs.